Meltdown

Mech Wars Book 3

Scott Bartlett

Mirth Publishing
St. John's

MELTDOWN

Cover art by: Tom Edwards (tomedwardsdesign.com)

This novel is a work of fiction. All of the characters, places, and events are fictitious. Any resemblance to actual persons living or dead, locales, businesses, or events is entirely coincidental.

Library and Archives Canada Cataloguing in Publication

Bartlett, Scott

Meltdown / Scott Bartlett ; illustrations by Tom Edwards.

ISBN 978-1-988380-09-4

To my father, Terry.

CHAPTER 1

All Combat Units

Ash stared at Chief Roach, and she realized that if she hadn't been inside her battered MIMAS mech, her mouth would have been hanging open.

"So, you...*dissolved?* You let that thing *eat* you?"

Roach stepped forward, his alien mech towering over the human-made MIMAS mechs. Except, Ash supposed it was no longer correct to think of it as "Roach's mech." If what he'd just said was true, the mech *was* Roach, in every sense.

"I wouldn't phrase it that way, exactly," he said. "The mech gave up as much as I did, Sweeney. It's bonded to me, now, permanently. It can't accept anyone else inside it, and it can never act on its own without me. If it tries to do something I don't like, I can veto that act, and vice versa."

"Wait, it can act on its *own?*"

Ash looked around at the other members of Oneiri Team—what members were present, anyway. Tommy was dead, Jake was gone, and Roach...

Is Roach even a member of Oneiri anymore? Ash wondered. That remained to be seen.

The other MIMAS mechs stood stock-still, as though unsure what to make of Roach, now, and unsure how to treat him. If Ash could have seen their expressions, she would have bet they'd feature a potent blend of shock, fear, and maybe even some revulsion.

She was certainly experiencing all of that herself. In equal measure.

Turning back to Roach, she said, "So, if you don't plan to lead us anymore, what do you plan on doing?"

Even though Roach was clearly able to have his metal body take virtually any shape, he'd kept all his weaponry active after the battle, and the mech bristled with it. It lent him a fearsome air. "I intend to continue doing exactly what I came down here to do—kill Quatro, along with anyone who tries to stop me from doing that. So don't get in my way."

Chief Roach—*Just Roach, now,* she reflected—turned as if to leave them, maybe to track down the remaining quads.

At that moment, Captain Arkady Black returned from his inspection of the surviving soldiers of the Winged Dragons. That was the Darkstream reserve battalion that had helped Oneiri Team wage the battle that had ended mere moments ago— against Quatro, Red Company mercenaries, and Quatro piloting quads.

"If that's the way it is, so be it, Roach," Black said. "Although, you haven't completed your current contract with Darkstream, and I expect the board of directors will have something to say about your defection."

Unexpectedly, Roach's laughter boomed across the plains of Eresos. "I no longer pay attention to the whimpering of corporate executives. They can come and whine at me all they like—I won't heed it. And if they think they have the power to reprimand me with anything beyond their inane babble, I invite them to try."

Black grunted. "Our aims align, at the moment, so I doubt they'll feel moved to put you down just yet. But if you're truly the rabid dog I suspect you've become, then that day *will* come. I hope you know that."

"Again...I invite it."

"Uh huh. Well, your business is your own. But before you leave, I hope you have enough humanity left in you to lend us your help in closing the tunnel the quads dug into Ingress. Surely you understand the danger of leaving it open—the danger to innocent people. We can close it much faster with your help."

For a long moment, Roach's midnight mech stood inert, seeming to stare at Black. Unless Ash missed her guess, Roach was glaring at the captain, and for a moment she expected him to refuse to lend his aid.

But she was wrong. "Very well," Roach said at last. "Let's make this quick."

"Yes, let's," Black said. "I'll accompany you to the hilltop where the tunnel begins, though I'm sure I can't keep up with a crowd of metal giants."

"On the contrary," Roach said. With that, he picked up Captain Black with one hand, whose face darkened with the indignity.

Roach's shoulder morphed to form a sort of saddle, which he deposited the captain into. Metal straps snaked out from either side of him to wrap around Black's legs and stomach, holding him fast.

"Come," Roach said, taking off across the terrain, toward the hill.

Exchanging glances with Beth, Ash followed, and so did the rest of Oneiri.

Paste, Ash thought. *That's the nickname I gave Beth.*

She'd given Marco one, too—*Spirit.* Surprisingly, no one had objected to the nicknames she'd doled out, even though she'd given Marco's sarcastically, and Paste...

Well, Paste is a serviceable nickname, I guess.

Before they reached the hilltop, Marco—Spirit—started thinking out loud. "There were eight quads that we know of, right? It's possible more came down in meteorites, but..."

He glanced at Ash, who nodded. "That's right, Marco. Eight, as far as we know."

"We took down one, and Chief Roach defeated two more. Before that, he chased off four. But that means there's still one unaccounted for. Doesn't it?"

Ash stopped running, and the rest of Oneiri Team did too, all of them turning to face her.

"Has anyone checked the tunnel since the battle?" she asked.

At that moment, an alert appeared in her vision, dominating her HUD.

It was from the Ingress garrison:

"INGRESS IS UNDER ATTACK! ALL DARKSTREAM COMBAT UNITS REPAIR TO THE CITY AT ONCE!"

"Come on!" Ash yelled, turning back to run toward Ingress. The other MIMAS mechs followed.

As she sprinted toward the city gates, she contacted the commander of the city garrison.

"It's a quad!" Cassandra Sora said, jogging alongside Ash inside the mech dream, looking completely freaked out. "It's only one of them, but nothing we're doing is having any effect. It's already slaughtered dozens of civilians. You need to get here, now!"

"We're on our way," Ash said, the dream translating the mech's exertion as a simulated ache in her own muscles. "Hold on as well as you can. We'll be there soon."

CHAPTER 2

Under Attack

For Lisa, the journey from Alex to Eresos had dragged on, seeming to last forever.

I wonder why, she thought sarcastically.

Maybe it was the fact that one of them needed to stay in the cockpit at all times, weapon in hand, to make sure the pilot followed the course they'd told him to follow. Lisa had instructed those in the other shuttles to do the same thing with their pilots.

Maybe it was the way Rug insisted on pacing up and down the craft, when there truly was no room for her to do that, especially with two other Quatro occupying the shuttle. Lisa had twitched every time the massive alien brushed her leg, and when Rug had bumped into Andy, Lisa snapped at her to lie down and stay there.

That brought her to the real reason the trip to Alex had seemed to take forever: Andy needed medical attention, and he needed it right now.

Lisa had done everything she could with what she'd found inside the shuttle's medkit, which was missing a lot of essential supplies. Apparently the pilot hadn't been performing his checks anywhere near as often as he should have.

Despite her efforts, a quick glance at Andy's vitals indicated he needed to see an actual doctor, as soon as possible.

You don't have to be a medical professional to figure that one out.

On her HUD, most of Andy's body was rimmed with red-tinged yellow, communicating sub-optimal health. His left leg, which now ended at the knee, terminated in a scarlet sun on Lisa's HUD, and his right leg was covered in maroon patches. A readout told her that the risk of infection was high, and the prophylactic antibiotics the medkit was supposed to contain had been one of the things missing due to the pilot's negligence.

"Tell dad I can prepare supper," Andy muttered. "I don't need him. I don't need the guilt trip. I'll do it."

Andy had fallen unconscious hours ago, and strangely, Lisa took solace in his occasional delirious muttering. It meant he was still alive; that his brain still functioned.

Other than monitoring his state using his vitals, all she could do was keep his forehead wet with water from a canteen she'd found in the back of the shuttle. She was doing everything she could to fight the fever that had already begun to form.

An hour before they reached Eresos, Lisa started getting updates from the system net about a battle that was underway just outside Ingress—the city where the space elevator terminated.

Of course. Of course there'd be a battle there now. It's not like we've faced enough problems.

The battle was between Darkstream troops on one side and Quatro on the other. Humans accompanied the Quatro, and some of the social posts had identified those humans as mercenaries.

The battle itself was being recorded by civilians who were documenting it from atop the city walls.

A few of the Quatro seemed to be piloting mechs of their own. Then, Lisa saw a video of yet another mech, this one a biped with similarities to those controlled by the aliens. It took on two of the Quatro mechs at once, and it won, even after the aliens ran it through with massive, razor-sharp lances.

Lisa didn't relay any of that to Rug. She didn't want to agitate the alien any more than she already was.

That changed when she received the alert from Ingress:

"INGRESS IS UNDER ATTACK! ALL DARKSTREAM COMBAT UNITS REPAIR TO THE CITY AT ONCE!"

Partly, she felt surprised to still be receiving alerts from Darkstream. *I guess they haven't gotten around to removing me from their database after what I did to Laudano and his soldiers. Or maybe they're just that desperate.*

Either way, she knew she now had to break her silence about the Quatro's involvement in the strife around Ingress.

"Rug," she said, and the alien's enormous head snapped up to look at her, quicker than Lisa would have thought it could move.

"Yes, Lisa?" she said. "Do you have news of my people on Eresos?"

Lisa hesitated. "I do, actually. I have news of one of them, anyway. And it's not good news, Rug."

"Tell me. Do not be hesitant."

"All right. Well, I've been keeping this from you—I'm sorry, but I thought it best, considering your agitation. Some of your people seem to have acquired mechs of their own, and one of them is rampaging through the streets of Eresos right now."

Rug regarded her silently, totally motionless. After several moments, Lisa began to wonder whether the Quatro had gone into shock.

Lisa cleared her throat. "Do you...do you think you can talk to it, Rug? Get it to stop, somehow?"

"I can try," Rug said, and she didn't speak again.

"Good," Lisa said, with a glance at Andy. *For a while, I thought things would become simpler once we reached Eresos. How stupid.* "That's all I ask, Rug—that you speak to it, and try to convince it to stop killing humans. Then, hopefully, we won't have to kill it."

CHAPTER 3

One Rocket Each

When Wound's tunnel broke through to the planet's surface, he emerged inside a cramped basement. Stone stairs led to an upper floor, though they were too narrow to accommodate him, and the door at the top was too small for him to pass through.

So he blasted it apart with a single shot from one of his energy cannons, leaving it a gaping, smoldering aperture.

Pouncing through, Wound came upon a frightened family sitting around a table, participating together in a meal. The largest, hairiest one of them got up, brandishing a small knife in its hand.

Is that a joke? The whispers asked from inside Wound.

He crossed the eating room in one stride and crushed the human with an enormous metal paw. Then he turned a low-caliber gun on the three that remained and put a swift end to them.

All four members of the family now lay strewn across the floor, having assumed the various twisted postures of death.

It's beautiful, the whispers remarked. *What a beautiful tapestry they make. Should we stay and admire it forever?*

"No," Wound muttered, and turned enormous energy cannons on one of the walls. He blasted it, causing it to disintegrate and reveal a narrow alley. Opposite the structure where he'd emerged sat another squat dwelling, over which hung an iron sky.

The weather's changing.

Just as were the fortunes of those humans that dwelled in this city.

The ones who benefited from the oppression of my brothers and sisters.

For a moment, that didn't seem like justification enough to proceed with the slaughter.

Don't I welcome the oppression of the Quatro? They deserve it, after all.

The whispers answered: *These humans have your mate somewhere in this settlement of steel and filth.*

"Ah," Wound muttered. "Yes."

He stalked out of the exit he'd created, following the alley toward a busier street, with vehicles the humans called speeders zipping back and forth along it. As Wound approached, a man and a woman passed the alley mouth as they progressed down the sidewalk.

His mech's heavy footfalls made them turn as he stepped onto the street, and they screamed, but Wound ignored them for now.

Yes. In addition to the speeders, there was also ample pedestrian traffic.

They will hear my demands. But first, I must teach them to listen.

Twin heavy machine guns projected suddenly from Wound's shoulders, even startling him a little. Inside the alien suit, his barest whim often manifested as dramatic physical phenomena.

Luckily, *this* phenomenon suited his purposes.

He sprayed the young, screaming couple with bullets, throwing them back to lie supine on the sidewalk—their bodies tattered, metal-ridden remnants.

Then, Wound galloped down that sidewalk, crushing any walkers too slow to get out of his way while firing rockets at the individual speeders; one rocket for each vehicle. The speeders lacked armor of any kind, and so one rocket seemed to do it; tossing them into each other, leaving massive dents in their metal bodies. Occasionally, the explosions were enough to tear the speeders open.

Before long, humans with guns came against him, seeking to stop his stampede, or maybe just to slow it.

They failed. Wound brought his energy cannons to bear once more, turning the puny creatures into scorched, smoldering lumps. He knew that if he used enough energy, he could cause them to disintegrate, just as he'd done to the walls of the structure he'd emerged inside. But he wanted to conserve his power, so that he could continue to attack until they gave him what he wanted.

What he *needed.*

"Where is my mate?" he bellowed as he rampaged through the city streets, across sidewalks and through roadways, firing energy at structures as often as he did at living beings, wrecking both. "Where is my *soul?*"

A Quatro emerged onto the street he charged along, from a lane that ran perpendicular to it. He'd been about to send an energy blast that way, but he reined himself in at the last instant.

"My love..." the Quatro said.

Wound took a stuttering step forward, and then he came to a halt, scrutinizing the female Quatro that had come before him.

"My...my soul?"

Part of him rejoiced at the sight of her, but another part couldn't seem to accept it. That part of him hadn't ever expected to find her here. Not really. That part knew that this killing spree had never truly been about finding her—it had been about something else entirely, something the whispers would reveal to him in time.

"It is I," she said.

"No," he said quietly. And then, much louder: "No!" He shook his head, trying to clear it. "You are not real. You are an impostor."

"It is truly I, my soul."

"Impossible! Your claim makes a mockery of my love's memory. She is gone, long gone, and there was never any hope of our reunion, except in my dreams. Do not cheapen my memories by attempting to trick me!"

"My love..."

"*No!*"

Wound turned, scrambling back the way he'd come, almost losing his footing as he fled.

Seeing his long-lost mate, real or not...for some reason, it had ruined everything he'd wanted to accomplish here. Her appearance meant he couldn't *be* here right now. It meant he needed to be far away, as soon as possible.

At last, after dashing through streets and lanes and alleyways, retracing his route with the help of his suit's HUD, he found the building where he'd first surfaced.

Wound leapt through the hole he'd made in the outer wall, and then he fled down the jagged mouth that had once been the door to the basement.

Wound fled back through the tunnel he'd dug.

CHAPTER 4

Swath of Destruction

As Gabe reached the bottom of the hill atop which the Quatro had started their tunnel, Ash appeared before him in the dream, looking harried. During remote communications, the dream rendered her as outside of her mech, and her face had paled, her short wheat-colored hair glistening with sweat.

"Sir. Did you get the alert?" she asked, somewhat breathless.

"What alert?"

"Ingress is under attack by a quad! It must have still been inside the tunnel all along."

"*Damn* it," Gabe spat, using his momentum to run up the incline, turn in a tight arc, and then head back toward the city.

"What's happening?" Captain Arkady Black asked, from where he still sat, strapped to Gabe's shoulder. "Why have we reversed direction?"

"There's a quad inside Ingress."

"I see. Let me down, then, Roach. I have to go meet the commander of the Ingress garrison."

"Negative. I don't intend to slow down, and at this speed, you'll be injured in the fall if I release you."

"I'm giving you an order, Chief!"

"And I'm ignoring it. I told you. I'm done with Darkstream."

"Darkstream isn't done with you," Black muttered darkly. "Of that, I can assure you."

Ingress' gates stood open, probably from the passage of the five MIMAS mechs piloted by Sweeney, Arkanian, Jin, Gonzalez, and Lafontaine. Gabe ran through, ignoring the guards who cried out in surprise as much as inquiry.

It didn't take long for him to find evidence of the quad's presence—buildings smashed open, blackened speeders lying belly-up on streets and sidewalks alike—and, worst of all, the charred remnants of human corpses.

The swath of destruction stretched in two directions, and after a brief study of the damage the alien had done, Gabe chose to sprint to his right, basing his decision on which way most of the scorch marks faced.

He didn't have long to go before finding something entirely unexpected. It was a Quatro, but one that wore no armor. Even though Gabe commanded his arms to take shape as massive energy cannons, his confusion caused him to hesitate momentarily, which saved the alien's life.

"Wait," it said, and the fact it could speak took Gabe aback even more. He'd known they must have had some way of communicating with the mercenaries—else, their alliance would have never come about, and even if it had, conducting it would have been a logistical nightmare.

Still, he hadn't expected to hear one of the beasts speak to him so plainly. And the way the thing had spoken to him had been deliberate, measured, even though it had only said one word, her tone ...

Intelligent. The analysis of both Gabe and his alien mech was that the being before him possessed a high degree of intelligence.

That's not going to do much for my nightmares of slaughtering Quatro. He still had those, and they tormented him even more, now that he spent every second inside the dream.

"Let me down," Black demanded, and Gabe did, rapidly generating a grasper smaller than the mech's regular hands to pluck the captain from his shoulder and set him on the ground, somewhat roughly.

With a brief glare for Gabe, Black headed down a nearby lane.

Gabe turned to the alien. "Are you the Quatro that was attacking this city?" he bellowed.

"I am not. But I just confronted the one that was, and he fled." The Quatro paused, then added: "He is known to me."

Gabe glared at the alien for a moment, his blood pounding hotly through his circulatory system, which was newly encased in metal. His brain ached.

Then, cursing, he ran straight toward the Quatro.

It braced itself against the ground, as though preparing for battle, and he screamed, "*Get out of my way!*"

The Quatro did, and he charged past, toward the city walls.

"Someone deal with that beast!" he yelled as he ran, hoping that members of the city garrison lingered nearby.

We can't allow a Quatro to roam the city, whether it's piloting a quad or not.

"Do not hurt him!" the Quatro called after Gabe, which surprised him all over again.

Does it really expect me to spare an enemy who slaughtered dozens of my own?

Just before reaching Ingress' wall, he ignited his launch thrusters, which carried his bulk up and over the towering barrier of steel. Atop it, a handful of civilians were using the wall as a viewing gallery, and their heads tracked Gabe's progress through the air.

Those directly below him would feel some of the heat of his passage, he knew.

Serves them right. Hopefully it will teach them to stand idly by while others fight, as though battle were some sort of spectator sport.

The exhaust wouldn't harm them, at this remove, so he considered the discomfort they would experience acceptable.

He came crashing down outside the city, hitting the ground running—straight for the hilltop, where he knew the quad would emerge.

The brittle, short-clipped grass blurred below him, and the hill grew quickly in his sight. It still shocked him to experience the sheer speed with which he could cross distances inside his new body.

He caught the quad just as it was scampering out of the tunnel, and he barreled into it, sending them both careening down the steep hill. They tumbled, rolled, and flipped down the incline, locked together by Gabe's death grip.

At the bottom of the hill, he managed to channel their momentum by bodyslamming the alien mech into the hard-packed ground, causing the earth to tremor.

As the alien regained its feet, Gabe willed his arms to become broadswords, and he adopted a ready stance, facing his adversary.

But the Quatro had no interest in fighting him. Instead, it retreated the moment it regained its feet, limping slightly at first, but quickly recovering.

Gabe cursed once again, ordering his broadswords to become energy turrets and sending white-hot threads across the plain to chase the quad.

But the Quatro randomized its path skillfully, and only one of the shots connected with it, causing it to stumble to the left before it recovered once again.

With that, the quad was gone, disappeared beyond a shallow rise near the horizon.

Gabe might have chased it, but it could have taken hours to catch up. Days, possibly. And he felt bound to return to Ingress and make sure the Quatro he'd left there hadn't harmed anyone else.

He turned toward the city again, vowing to find the quad that had escaped him, and to make it pay.

CHAPTER 5

The Beast

"Clear," Lisa said over the militia-wide channel, which was the signal for the other half of her fighters, led by Tessa Notaras, to leapfrog ahead of her own squad to scout the next street while Lisa's squad provided covering fire.

Lisa swept everything she could see with her assault rifle's scope while keeping a close eye on her HUD, which would represent enemy units with red squares the moment she or one of her soldiers identified them.

Other than Rug, all the Quatro remained with the shuttles. They were too big to fit inside the cockpits, but they were perfectly capable of crouching just outside them with energy weapons trained on the Darkstream pilots, who'd been informed that any wrong moves would result in their summary deaths.

Andy's back there, too. Andy, whose infection was festering. *I won't let you die. Not when we're this close.*

By using the leapfrogging technique, they were able to move safely and fairly swiftly. Before long, Tessa's squad spotted Rug surrounded by five of Darkstream's new **MIMAS** mechs. The

HUD colored Rug in yellow, and a second after that, Tessa patched through a visual feed as well.

But Lisa wanted to see her friend with her own eyes. She ordered her squad to proceed with caution as she slowly advanced herself.

One of the mech's heads turned toward her as she approached, seeming to see her coming. Underneath the patina of battle damage each mech bore, they all had differing designs. This one had yellow swirls covering its face and body.

"You're Lisa Sato," the mech said in a feminine voice, which sounded like it belonged to someone Lisa's age.

"I am," Lisa said. "Who are you?"

"Seaman Apprentice Ash Sweeney. But that's not your concern right now. What's of much greater concern is why you've entered Ingress without permission from the Darkstream garrison, accompanied by this *Quatro* with whom you appear to be allied."

"We skipped customs because we thought we could prevent that Quatro mech from killing more people. Also, we have someone in our party in dire need of medical attention." Lisa cleared her throat, struggling to meet the giant robot's gaze. She was certain the mech's visage had been designed to appear both menacing and impersonal at the same time. "As for my Quatro friend, whose name is Rug, she saved my life, along with forty-one of her brethren. Those same Quatro helped us to retake Habitat 2 from criminals. Most of the ones who helped us are now dead, but those that remain have accompanied us here."

"Yes, they accompanied you inside shuttles you hijacked from our mutual employer," Sweeney said, her voice cold. "Tell me: did these Quatro also help you kill Commander Laudano and his soldiers? There's a warrant out for your arrest, Lisa Sato."

Lisa had no answer for that. How could she make this metal-clad company loyalist understand the necessity of defeating Laudano?

Lisa almost laughed at herself. *Company loyalist. She's no different than I was, mere days ago.* "Commander Laudano conspired with Quentin Cooper—the leader of a criminal gang called Daybreak—to consign the residents of Habitat 2 to slavery."

Now, it was the mech pilot's turn to fall silent, and the mech itself remained perfectly still. Near her, one of the other mechs twitched, which Lisa interpreted as shock at the specter she'd just raised.

But do they accept it as truth? She knew it couldn't possibly be that easy. *Nevertheless, we must try.*

Without warning, a larger, darker mech charged out of a side alley, tackling Rug with a jagged shoulder and sending the massive alien flying to crash into a nearby office building.

"*No!*" Lisa cried, sprinting forward to place herself between Rug and the strange mech, who she recognized from the system net vids of the recent battle. She raised her palms toward it.

"Get out of my way," a deep voice boomed as the mech's arms became massive cannons, inside which energy began to collect and coalesce. That voice, while recognizable as human, was stripped of everything connected to humanity.

Its owner has endured incredible torment. That, Lisa knew straight away.

"I will not," she said, proud that her voice shook only slightly.

"Gabriel Roach," Tessa called, her own voice totally firm. "Is that you inside that bucket?"

Slowly, the alien mech turned to face Tessa, not lowering its energy cannons by a centimeter. "Tessa Notaras," it growled, working through the words as though they were mouthfuls of taffy. "You *dare* return here?"

"Only for great need."

"I told you *never* to return. Because of the evil you helped perpetrate. Have you come back to do more evil?"

"I've come to help finally correct it." Tessa stepped toward the mech, looking much more resolute than Lisa thought she herself could have managed. "You want to talk evil, Roach? Let's talk about our employer, who you've continued to work for."

"I don't work for them anymore."

Raising her eyebrows, Tessa said, "That must be a very recent development, then. Because for seventeen years, you remained in the employ of the beast who ordered me to perpetrate the very evil you banished me for. I was blind to that hypocrisy, then—blinded by guilt. But since leaving for Alex, I've had a *long* time to think about what happened between us. Darkstream is profit-mad, and its main vehicle for profit is an expanding campaign of exploitation and terror. It's always been that way, and recently it's gotten much worse. They've already enslaved the population of Habitat 2. Next, they'll certainly do the same to everyone on Alex. But it all started here, didn't it?

With their genocide of the Quatro, who we both know aren't the demons they tricked everyone into thinking they were. Not even close."

"A Quatro killed the only woman I ever loved," Roach said, and for the first time, Tessa was visibly taken aback.

So Lisa spoke up, addressing Roach. "The Quatro you just attacked, Rug, is certain her brethren were provoked into war."

The alien mech shook its head. "Even if I accepted that, I would never work with someone as duplicitous as you, Tessa. The news that you helped murder Commander Laudano and his soldiers only makes me more sure about you."

Tessa spat on the pavement, then turned her glare on Roach once more. "Your interpretation of *everything* is incredibly convenient for you, Roach. Why am I not surprised?" She leveled a finger at the alien mech's head, which involved angling her arm at quite an incline. "You obviously don't intend to help us in any way. But I know there's a voice inside of you, telling you that there's something wrong with the way you see things, and something very right about how I've explained them. So, tell me: is that voice loud enough for you to understand you *must* let us leave this city? Or will you attempt to apprehend us in spite of it?"

A long moment passed, with Roach and Tessa locked in a silent combat of will.

At last, Roach said, "Get out of my sight. If I see you again, I'll kill you."

Tessa looked at Lisa, subvocalizing: "Let's get back to the shuttles. I don't know how long this offer will last."

Nodding, Lisa got on the militia-wide. "Let's move, everyone. Back to the shuttles, double-time."

CHAPTER 6

Good and Evil

With the alien mech safely neutralized, contained, and onboard the *Javelin*, Bronson was driving his crew hard to complete preparations for their departure from the Belt as soon as possible.

Nothing was expected of Jake, however. Bronson had permitted him to pay his father a short visit aboard the *Whale*, to say goodbye.

Evidently, the visit could have been longer.

Right now, Jake was sitting in the Starlight Lounge with absolutely nothing to do, and had been for a while.

He still remembered the day Bronson had first brought him here. Before then, he'd never been anywhere outside the Belt. His main concern had been making enough money for Sue Anne to get the treatment she needed—well, that was still his main concern, actually. But back then, his life had been confined to the *Whale* and the endless series of comets they'd developed for homesteaders eager to put as much distance as possible between themselves and civilization.

The idea that the inner Steele System constituted "civilization" would have seemed odd to anyone from the Milky Way—Jake knew that. This entire system was basically the frontier, perhaps in the truest sense of the word since ancient Europeans had first colonized North America.

But to Jake, the inner system *did* mean civilization, with its cities, its space station, and its ever-expanding industrial base.

And since walking into the Starlight Lounge to be wowed by Bronson's promises of mech combat, glory, and riches, he'd seen that civilization for himself.

Despite it all, he missed the Belt. He missed Hub; the closest thing the Belt had to a city, and also the place Jake was from. Perhaps most of all, he missed life out here with his father, hopping from comet to comet, pining for something else, without ever realizing he already had everything he needed.

I was so naive.

He'd been convinced, that the Ixa could arrive at any time, to finish off the remnants of humanity—or maybe one of the species would show up from the systems that surrounded Steele, which did show signs of occupation by intelligent life. Jake had believed he *needed* to join the Darkstream military, to use what he'd learned from lucid to navigate training, and to rack up combat experience. To become mighty, so that when aliens did attack, he could act like some big hero.

He'd believed that everything would always be simple, that he would always consider himself good and his enemies evil.

But as he sat here with his hands wrapped around a cup of cold tea, it wasn't like that at all. He felt empty, with nothing but the blood on his hands and the indoctrination Darkstream's training had left him with.

The handful of crewmembers that were inside the lounge kept their distance from Jake. He could tell they considered him an "other"—a mech pilot, who'd been given a shiny new toy, and who'd recently done battle with a fearsome alien robot.

If he were to guess, he'd say the crews' feelings toward him entailed a mixture of fear and resentment. The way Bronson lavished praise and privilege on him didn't help. Possibly, that was an innocent impulse on the captain's behalf, though Jake doubted it. Nothing was ever innocent with Bronson. More likely, he did it to keep Jake apart from the crew.

Divide and conquer. That was the secret Darkstream mantra, he'd come to realize.

He decided to browse the system net, to see whether he could find any news about the situation on Eresos.

Scrolling through one of his social feeds, amidst the posts about everyday life, he saw a smattering of rumors that Quatro in mechs of their own were approaching Ingress. Because of the signal delay, that news would be several hours stale, and it would be some time before he'd find out how Ash and the others had truly fared.

That killed him—the not knowing.

Idly, he refreshed his feed, and the post that appeared at the top caused him to bolt up from his chair, eyes riveted on the rectangle in the upper right of his HUD, which displayed the social feed.

A few of the crewmembers glanced toward him before returning to their drinks, but Jake ignored them, rereading the post:

"Attention to anyone near Hub: we are under attack. Strange robots have infiltrated our comets and have begun attacking us. We've contacted Darkstream but haven't heard back. If you're reading this and are able to help, please, please come."

Willing the social feed to dissolve, Jake tore out of the Starlight Lounge and sprinted toward Bronson's office, which was just a short distance down the corridor. He pounded on the hatch while sending Bronson IM after IM.

Finally, the hatch opened to reveal Bronson, whose eyes were underscored with black patches. "Price. What can I do for you?"

"Hub is under attack."

Bronson inclined his head. "I've heard. It's unfortunate, but sadly we can't alter our itinerary."

"Our *itinerary?* People are dying!"

"I'm afraid it's out of the question, Price. We need all hands on deck back on Eresos. The situation there has gone completely to pot."

Jake squinted at Bronson, unsure whether the captain had gone mad or he had. "To pot...?" He shook his head to clear it. "My family is in Hub, sir!"

Shoulders rising slightly before falling again, Bronson said softly: "This is what it means to be a soldier, son."

"I see," Jake said, and suddenly, he felt totally at peace. Something had fallen into place, and with it, everything had begun to make a lot more sense. Amazingly, the captain's words had soothed many of his woes, and they'd done that by simplifying things for him. He knew exactly what he had to do.

"Are you going to be all right, son?"

"I'm going to be fine, sir," Jake said.

"Okay, then. Well, if you ever need to talk, we have a fine doctor aboard."

"Yes, sir."

"Good man." Bronson cleared his throat. "Dismissed, Price."

But as the captain was saying the words, Jake was already turning to leave.

CHAPTER 7

Sucker Punch

It's beautiful.

Lisa had heard a lot of old-timers say that Eresos came nowhere near the custom-tailored planets of human space back in the Milky Way, and certainly it would have paled beside the natural beauty of Old Earth, though no one alive had ever seen that, outside of ancient photos.

Lisa didn't care what people said, anyway. For someone who had lived most of her life in the Belt, and then the rest of it on barren Alex, Eresos seemed downright lush—even with its leafless trees, its mildew smell, and the sweeping Barrens she'd heard about but hadn't seen yet.

Of course, Hub does *give it a run for its money.* Like the terraformed planets back in the Milky Way, Hub had also been carefully designed and cultivated to please the eye, using plants cloned from heritage seeds that had been salvaged from humanity's homeworld.

But Eresos was...natural. Natural, which was supposed to be the reason for Old Earth's striking beauty. She'd read once that humans had evolved to find the landscapes of Earth's savannas appealing, with their winding water sources; their open plains that had enabled ancient humans to run down prey; and their scattered copses, perfect for hiding from predators...

"Tessa," she said, and the older woman's gaze drifted toward her slowly, as though she'd been expecting to be addressed.

"Yes, Lisa?"

"The man inside the alien mech—Roach. What did he mean when he mentioned the 'evil' you helped to bring about? Why did he call you duplicitous?"

For a long time, Tessa returned her stare in silence.

Next to Lisa, Andy's shallow breathing was ragged though steady, and the two Quatro on the floor—Rug, and one who'd chosen the name Nail—seemed to take little interest in their conversation, though Lisa had a hunch that Rug, who she knew best, was in fact listening.

When Tessa's reply came , it was subvocalized. "Let's meet in lucid."

Lisa nodded, maintaining eye contact while she slipped out a sedative and ingested it. In the crash seat across from hers, Tessa did the same.

The dream soon enveloped Lisa, and she found herself in the lobby which she'd set her implant to put her in by default. She accepted Tessa's invitation when it came.

An instant later, she found herself walking along a mountain pass, with Tessa beside her. They stood in the middle of a landscape filled with mountains that stretched from horizon to horizon. As beautiful as the mountains were in height and breadth, that was not their most striking feature: rainbows seemed to cover each mountain. Some mountains only bore two colors in alternating lines, and others had more. Lisa spotted one that had at least five distinct hues.

Most of the colors were various shades of red and brown, though she also saw yellow, white, blue, gray, and black.

"Did you...make this?" Lisa said, her voice hitching as her breath caught in her throat.

"No," Tessa said. "This was the Zhangye Danxia region, in ancient China. I don't know what it looks like now, after the Degradation, but someone captured its likeness in virtual reality for all time, and now we get to visit it."

"How did you come to learn of it?"

"I read about it in a book."

Lisa nodded. *Of course. Tessa reads about everything in a book.*

Suddenly, she turned toward her friend as she felt a scowl tighten her mouth and brow. "Wait. I know what you're doing, Tessa Notaras."

Tessa was ahead of her on the trail, and now she stopped walking in order to turn toward Lisa, eyebrows raised, her face the very picture of innocence.

But Lisa wasn't fooled.

"You want me awestruck and lightheaded, don't you? I can taste how realistically the dream has rendered this mountain air. This is the state of mind you want me in as you tell me what Roach was talking about. It must have been quite bad, if that's the case."

For a few moments more, Tessa maintained her veneer of purity and surprise. Then, she dropped the act. "I should never have taught you as much as I have," she muttered.

"Enough stalling," Lisa said. "Enough tricks. Tell me what he was talking about."

Shoulders rising and falling more quickly, now, Tessa said, "Yes. Okay. Do you remember all those times you asked me what, exactly, Darkstream had done to make me mistrust them so?"

"Yes..."

"And do you remember how I'd always refuse to tell you?"

"You said that you would, someday."

"Today is that day. And the reason I couldn't tell you before what the awful thing Darkstream did was because *I helped them do it.*"

Lisa crossed her arms. "Go on."

With a long sigh, Tessa continued: "Captain Bronson—Commander Bronson, back then—was in command of the first missions to Eresos, the stated aim of which was to secure a new home for humanity. Unfortunately, Eresos already had someone living on it."

"The Quatro," Lisa said.

"Yes. One of them attacked us, or at least, it seemed to. I now think that attack was provoked by Mario Laudano. Either way, it wasn't enough to rile the troops like Bronson wanted them riled. So he enlisted me to help him create the fiction that the Quatro control the Amblers, and that they'd ordered one of them to attack us, killing some of our soldiers. It was only by chance that the Ambler attacked, of course, but I helped Bronson make the others think the Quatro ordered it."

Lisa uncrossed her arms, and now she let her hands dangle at her sides. Her shoulders slumped a little. "How did you do that?"

"I lured one of the Amblers near the entrance to a Quatro cave, to make it look like it was defending them, just as three platoons led by Bronson were closing in. They defeated the Ambler, and we lost more soldiers doing so. After the deaths of their comrades, the rest were enraged enough to kill the Quatro in their homes."

Hesitating for a moment, Lisa said, "But...but no one thinks the Quatro control the Amblers, now."

"No. Eventually, the soldiers realized the truth. But by then, they had so much Quatro blood on their hands, they couldn't look reality in the face. I think most of them suppressed the realization. And of the soldiers that survived the conquest of Eresos—the ones that didn't commit suicide afterward, or consign themselves to reclusion in the Belt—I've never heard any of them mention that they once thought the Quatro owned the Amblers."

"Why did you do it, Tessa? How did Bronson convince *you* to help trick the others?"

Now, Tessa's gaze sunk, until it fell on the pebbled trail where they stood. "He convinced me that doing so would prevent more deaths, in the long run. That if we could rally the soldiers to attack the Quatro—who were clearly vicious, he said— then we'd stop them from hitting us when we least expected it. Bronson said that I *needed* to help him, in order to atone."

"Atone?"

Another labored sigh leaked from Tessa's lips. "Have you ever heard of the catastrophe that preceded the Battle for Larkspur-Caprice, back in the Milky Way? When hundreds of thousands of UHF members were killed by wormholes that were sabotaged by Ochrim, the Ixan?"

"Yes," Lisa said haltingly. "I've heard the story."

"Well, *I'm* the one who let Ochrim access the wormhole master control. I was head of security for Darkstream headquarters at the time. Ochrim was our Chief Science Officer."

"Tessa...surely you can't blame yourself for what an *Ixan* set out himself to do."

"I've come to terms with my involvement. In a fashion. But that day still haunts my nightmares."

Lisa lowered herself onto a boulder at the side of the path, resting her hands on her knees, gazing out over the breathtaking landscape. What Tessa had just related to her had amounted to an emotional sucker punch. She'd known since their exchange with Roach in Ingress that whatever Tessa had been keeping from her, it had to be bad. But she hadn't quite expected this.

At last, Lisa peered up at Tessa, who was still standing. "How will we explain this to Rug?"

"Well...I was hoping not to. At least, not until we've stopped Darkstream. This could drive a rift between us and our alien friends, Lisa—potentially one we aren't able to close."

"Okay," Lisa said, her voice coming out softer than she'd intended. "If you want to keep this from Rug, that's your right. But you should know that I think it's wrong."

With that, Lisa held Tessa's gaze for several long moments before exiting the dream.

CHAPTER 8

Phantoms

Gabe stalked through the streets of Ingress, casting his gaze into every street, alley, or nook large enough to hold a Quatro.

An empty lot opened up on his right, and he turned abruptly, ready to unleash rockets he'd had the mech manufacture hours ago.

Nothing. So far, anyway.

"Sir…"

Gabe whirled around to face Ash Sweeney, who trailed him inside her MIMAS a few meters back. "What?" he snapped.

"We've been searching for hours. We already know from the spaceport footage that only one Quatro got off those shuttles, and the shuttles have long departed."

"There might have been others inside the tunnel the Quatro dug. They could be in hiding." He turned, resuming his search. "And stop calling me sir."

At first, all five MIMAS mechs remaining on Eresos had followed him throughout the city. Eventually, though, they'd taken him up on his repeated invitations to go away. All except Sweeney.

At the start of his search, he'd occasionally come across residents of the city, who'd just been starting to emerge after the quad's attack.

Now, he encountered no one. Word of his search had no doubt spread, probably via the system net, and the residents were staying indoors.

He spared a moment to consider how he must look to them. A shape-shifting alien monstrosity, ranging up and down the streets, looking for...

For what? A phantom. The Quatro are gone.

Yet he kept looking.

It occurred to him that if he could have gotten Jess back somehow—not as a hallucination, but as a flesh-and-blood woman—he would appear monstrous to her. It was ridiculous to entertain the idea that they'd be able to have any sort of life together, now. They wouldn't be able to hold each other, or to express their affection physically in any way.

It doesn't matter. I'll never get her back. The best I'll get is vengeance, and this thing *is what I've become in the pursuit of that.*

So he kept looking.

"Sir," Ash said, "what Tessa Notaras said about Darkstream..."

"Notaras is a liar of the worst sort. She should be behind bars."

Ash didn't answer right away, and for a time the only sound was the *clank-clank* of their metal feet on asphalt.

"Even so," she said at last. "It takes a lot of guts to tell a lie of that magnitude—to shout it with as much conviction as she did, in front of as many witnesses as were gathered. Have you considered that it might be true?"

Of course it could be true. Like so many others in the Steele System, Gabe had been in denial for a long time about the company upon which their society was based. In order for people to confront the truth, they'd have to acknowledge that what prosperity there was wouldn't have been possible without the crimes and atrocities regularly committed by Darkstream.

Having parted ways with the company, Gabe was finally beginning to reckon with the crimes he'd enabled, as well as the ones he'd committed himself while in Darkstream's employ. A little, at least. But ultimately, whether what Tessa had said was true didn't matter, because it was irrelevant to his quest for vengeance. As long as Darkstream didn't get in the way of *that,* they had nothing to fear from him.

"Sir?" Sweeney said. And then, much softer: "Dynamo?"

"Notaras is a liar and a criminal," Gabe snapped. "That's all I have to say on the subject. And don't call me that name."

"You're still a part of Oneiri Team, sir. Whether you like it or not. You created us."

He didn't answer, though he increased his pace, hoping she would finally stop following.

"I know you're hurting," Sweeney went on. "I'm hurting, too. What matters is that we work together...to win. That's the best way to honor the lives of the people we've lost."

Gabe drew to a stop, and he stayed there—completely motionless in the middle of the street.

"Sir?" From the proximity of her voice, he could tell Sweeney had drawn close behind him.

Whirling, Gabe willed his hands to become a single fist.

He sent that fist straight into Sweeney's solar plexus. Her mech's feet left the ground, and she flew through the air to crash to the asphalt on her back, at least twenty meters away.

"Stop following me," he ground out. "And stop talking to me. Never do either of those things, in fact. Ever again."

He turned to march away, not looking back.

Is our union that which nullifies? asked a voice whose tone dripped with hidden meaning.

Gabe's head jerked involuntarily, but he remained focused on his search.

He hadn't heard that voice since before the battle with the quads outside Ingress.

It had returned, it seemed.

You're doing well, it said.

Gabe ignored the voice, and it didn't speak again.

CHAPTER 9

Sympathy for O'Toole

Lisa felt like she had a lot to process, as she watched Eresos pass by on the viewscreen she'd made the pilot turn on for them.

Learning the truth about Tessa's past had messed with her head, and she wasn't sure what bothered her more—the things her friend had done or the fact that Tessa had never told her about them, despite how close they were.

But she had to shove that out of her mind. There were more pressing matters to consider.

Like what the hell we're going to do now.

"We didn't even come close to convincing those mech pilots to join us," she said to the others in the shuttle, thinking out loud for the benefit of their commentary.

"That does not matter," Rug said, lifting her massive head from her paws. "Does it? We still have the footage of Darkstream's deeds on Alex, including the confession Mario

Laudano volunteered when he thought we could not possibly escape him."

"It *does* matter," Tessa said, and though she spoke confidently, she'd lost some of her usual bravado. "If we don't have the muscle to bring Darkstream to justice, it won't matter if we release the footage. It will embarrass them, and it may even cost them money. But it won't topple them. Not by itself. It'll only piss them off."

Lisa nodded. "Tessa's right. We need allies, and I'm guessing the other Darkstream soldiers will be about as unlikely to join us as the mech pilots. That means we need to start locating Quatro drifts."

Andy moaned wordlessly, drawing Lisa's gaze.

Just before they'd left Ingress, Lisa had grabbed a medkit from one of the other shuttles. Once she had it aboard, she discovered that the pilot in charge of keeping it replenished had also been negligent, and the only antibiotics she could scrounge from it consisted of two large blue pills.

She'd dissolved them in water and gently poured them down Andy's throat. That had caused him to gag, at first, which she considered a positive sign.

They'd seemed to take effect quickly, and within hours his fever had dropped, along with his nonsensical muttering.

But she'd only found two pills, and once they wore off, Andy's condition began to worsen again. Now, his muttering had turned into wordless moans, and he thrashed about in his crash seat. If it hadn't been for the straps holding him there, he would have thrown himself onto the shuttle's deck.

Unable to take it anymore, Lisa ripped off her own straps to storm across the craft, past the Quatro whose energy weapon was trained on the pilot, and into the cockpit.

"Land the shuttle," she said.

The pilot turned to blink at her. "Pardon?"

"You heard me. I want you to land. Now." Her fingers found her pistol's grip, and she caressed it.

"It isn't safe," the pilot said, eyes flitting to her firearm. "There are mercenaries and Quatro fighting Darkstream all over the place. I even spotted one of those quadruped mechs. I'm not landing."

Lips pursed, Lisa shook her head. "Are you trying to tell me that every square inch of Eresos is covered in fighting mercenaries and aliens?"

"Um..." The pilot sniffed, and his Adam's apple bobbed as he swallowed.

"That's what I thought. Now that we have *that* cleared up, you'll do exactly as I say. Put this shuttle down within five minutes or suffer the consequences." Eyebrows raised, she patted the butt of the pistol.

"Militia members," Lisa said over the channel they'd agreed on before leaving Alex. "I need everyone to search their shuttle's medkits for antibiotics. If you find some, report to me. I need one of you to have your pilot land as soon as mine does, so that I can get the medication from you. It's for Andy. He's in rough shape." Through the cockpit's open hatch, Lisa stared at Andy's pale, sweaty face, and she frowned.

Maybe I should have turned him over to Darkstream back at Ingress...just so he could have gotten the attention he needs.

But no. Andy wouldn't have wanted that. She was pretty sure he would rather die than become Darkstream's prisoner, after what he'd seen the company do back on Alex.

Ten minutes later, she was stepping out of her shuttle's airlock onto a meadow full of tall, brittle grass that waved in the wind. She shielded her eyes to watch another shuttle swoop in to land gently next to hers.

Bob O'Toole stepped out of the airlock, grinning like a fool.

"Why the smile, O'Toole?" Lisa asked, her tone flat. "Are you happy to be deep behind enemy lines, with limited fuel and supplies?"

"I'm just happy to get to see your pretty face."

She marched over to him, snatched the medkit, and wrenched it open. Its contents fell out onto the grass, and she sifted through them with her boot until she found what she needed.

Plucking up a transparent, yellow-tinted bottle, she held it up to the sunlight. *Cefoxitin.* That was what she'd given Andy before, and it had seemed to work wonders. *Perfect.*

"Did you find what you need?" Tessa asked as she emerged from the shuttle behind Lisa, squinting into the sun.

"Who's watching the pilot?" Lisa asked.

"Rug just took over. Don't worry. I'm pretty sure if she could fit inside the cockpit, that energy gun of hers would be squarely up his ass."

Lisa suspected she was supposed to laugh at that, but she wasn't in the mood for comedy at present.

"Hey, it was kind of funny," she said when Tessa's smile faded from her face, replaced by a grim expression.

Then, she realized that Tessa was staring at something. She followed her friend's gaze to the horizon, where several large, purple shapes were striding toward them, the grass parting around their massive frames.

"Looks like we found our first drift," Tessa said.

The Quatro must have seen them land, because they headed directly for the two shuttles parked side-by-side.

"Should we get out of here?" Bob O'Toole said, his voice quavering.

"No," Lisa said. "We're looking for Quatro. Remember?"

"Sure," he said. "But now that I see them coming, I'm not so sure I want to find them, anymore. At least, not unless with the rest of the militia at my back, fully armed, with a few bazookas for good measure."

"It's hard to make friends with bazookas, O'Toole," Tessa said. "Although, maybe this explains why you don't have any. Friends, that is."

Lisa was surprised at the pang of pity she felt for O'Toole at Tessa's words. It was standard Tessa ribbing, but O'Toole was such a pathetic target that the comment rang a little too true.

I must be tired. Sympathy for O'Toole was the last thing she would have expected to feel.

When the Quatro reached them, they arranged themselves in a broad arc, all of them facing Lisa.

A few seconds passed while both species stared at each other.

Then, without warning, one of the giant aliens emitted a wordless roar and charged straight at Tessa.

CHAPTER 10

Until I Am Satisfied

By the collective!

When Rug saw the Quatro approaching across the field, her spirits soared. She asked Nail to watch the pilot for her again, and ever-agreeable, Nail agreed. Rug went straight to the airlock.

That turned out to be a fateful decision.

Her joy at the prospect of reuniting with long-lost kin turned to ashes in her mouth as one of the Quatro surged toward Tessa Notaras, just as the outer airlock door was opening.

Rug burst from the cramped chamber, meeting the Quatro just before he reached her friend. That encounter likely would have ended with death for Tessa—a lone human stood almost no chance against a Quatro, not unless they piloted one of their great machines.

Tessa did not pilot one, and so Rug's timing was fortuitous. The Quatro was halted in its tracks, but Rug did not stop there—not without making sure her friends were safe, first.

She continued charging forward, toppling the Quatro until he fell to the grass with a crash. Rug placed a paw on his chest, extending her claws so that he would feel their pricks.

"It appears I have the best of you, *friend*," she said, panting slightly.

"Your might serves the drift well...friend."

"Today, my might has spared a friend of us both. This human has done many good works. Why did you attack her?"

At that, the strange Quatro's lips drew back into a snarl, and he hissed. "That is no friend of ours. She is responsible for hundreds of Quatro deaths."

Rug hesitated. *Could there be some error?*

She decided this warranted further investigation. "If I release you, will you promise to relent until I am satisfied?"

"Yes."

Rug removed her paw, and her fellow Quatro rose to his feet, glaring at Tessa.

Pausing to gather her thoughts, Rug also met Tessa's gaze. The humans would not have understood the exchange that had just transpired. Rug had not activated her translator, since it would only have spoken over her, muddying the conversation.

"This one claims that you were responsible for Quatro deaths, Tessa Notaras." she said. "Is that true?"

Her words had a strange effect on the human. Tessa went rigid, and the color drained from her face. Although Rug still hadn't figured out human body language completely, she surmised that this reaction likely served as confirmation.

Her spirits sank even farther.

"It's true," Tessa said at last, her eyes wide.

Rug didn't answer. Instead, she approached Tessa slowly, the grass rustling under her paws with each step.

Soon, she towered over the human, glaring down at her. And for a long moment, she did not know what her own reaction would be.

But then she turned back toward the Quatro she'd just met. "Tell me more of this travesty."

"With pleasure," the Quatro growled. "This human led many attacks on the meager dwellings the Quatro took for themselves on this forsaken planet. Even when the first drift to encounter the two-legs offered a deep gesture of peace, they responded with aggression. And this human's face is etched into my mind forever. Most of my old drift is now dead thanks to an attack that she led."

Rug swung her head toward Tessa, whose posture was so much different from what Rug was used to seeing from the human. Normally, Tessa conducted herself with confidence—or at least, as far as Rug could tell, based on her limited understanding of human social interaction.

Now, Tessa looked...well, she looked guilty. As though her spirit had shrunk as small as her body.

"This is a deep betrayal," Rug said.

"Rug—" Tessa began, and her voice broke off, full of emotion. She began again: "Rug, there is more to this. There's no excuse for what I did, but I can at least offer you the reasons I had for doing it."

"I will hear them, Tessa Notaras. Because of the respect I held for you before today, I will hear them. But not now. Now, we have urgent business, and I'm afraid you can no longer be trusted to conduct it."

"You speak to them with facility," said the Quatro who'd nearly killed Tessa Notaras.

"Yes," Rug said. "Our fortunes have been aligned for some time." For a moment, emotion threatened to overcome her, but she forced herself to press on. "We have come to uncover the truth about this war. I have always known the Quatro would not fight so fiercely unless provoked, and you have confirmed that. Now, all that remains is to find a way to defeat this Darkstream."

The Quatro sat back on its haunches, his gaze never leaving Rug's. "The Quatro in this region are already locked in furious combat with that force for evil. We have found allies in some of the humans—and so we know that not all of them are rotten— but I am saddened to report that we have just suffered a major defeat. I do not believe we have the forces required to win."

"Have you given up hope so easily, friend?"

"No," the Quatro said. "I said we lack the necessary forces in *this* region. But there is a region across the Barrens, far to the east, where many Quatro have ventured but none have returned. I am convinced there must be many more drifts of Quatro there."

"We have craft to speed our journey," Rug said. "If you truly believe this, and are willing to join actions to your words, then perhaps, together, this we can achieve."

"I will come—partly in penance for disrespecting you. I attacked one of your party without first engaging you, and for that I apologize."

Rug did not mention the fact that this Quatro had not even known she was aboard the shuttle until she'd emerged. She did not mention it, since she would be just as remorseful in his place.

"You say you are receptive to the idea that not all humans are rotten. Would you also receive one of my human friends into the care of your drift? He is near death."

"I will lobby my brothers and sisters on his behalf. They are sure to agree to it. It is the Quatro way, is it not? Despite everything else, that is still true. With luck, he will recover in our absence. No doubt our allies among the Red Company will be able to help."

"Red Company—these are the human allies you mentioned?"

"Indeed."

Rug turned back to her human companions. "These Quatro will see that Andy gets the care he needs." She swung her head to meet Lisa Sato's gaze. "Based on my discussion with my new friend, it seems our highest chances of success await to the east."

Lisa nodded. "I trust your judgment, Rug. You can explain the plan while we're in transit. O'Toole, get Andy out of the shuttle. Will you stay with him?"

O'Toole nodded. "Anything for you, sweetheart. Andy might be a cocky brat, but he was always willing to have a drink with me. Besides, Phineas would have stayed with him. So I will, too."

"Thank you, O'Toole." Lisa turned back to Rug, and Rug found her expression just as inscrutable as she had found Tessa's. "Rug...are we okay? Is everything going to be okay, between us?"

"Nothing could mar our friendship, Lisa Sato." *Nothing, except learning that you slaughtered my people in droves.*

"I feel the same way," Lisa said. She appeared to draw a great breath. "We'd better get started."

CHAPTER 11

Emergency Bulletin

The grass of Eresos crunched underfoot as Ash trailed behind Beth.

She gave a pleasurable sigh, which drew a smile from the other young woman.

It's been too long.

It felt good to experience the world with her own body, after so long inside her **MIMAS**. To feel actual sunbeams play across her skin, and not a sun simulated by the dream. To breathe actual air, instead of oxygen that had been piped to her by her mech.

To live life unmediated by a walking metal weapon.

Currently, their mechs were being repaired of the damage they'd endured since first deploying to Eresos. Ash's in particular was being fitted with a new bayonet, since one of hers had been snapped during the recent battle.

Typically, she felt vulnerable outside her **MIMAS**, unprotected by its armor and weapons. But with the city walls in sight, atop which the garrison of Ingress watched over them, she could breathe easier than she normally might have while clad only in clothes.

Besides, lately, she'd been feeling vulnerable even *inside* her MIMAS. The mechs Darkstream had engineered, while more formidable than any ground combat unit ever deployed by humanity, were no match for the quads piloted by the Quatro, and she feared the bipedal alien mech that Chief Roach piloted would make short work of her, if they ever found themselves on opposite sides.

The memory of the way Roach had thrown her backward several meters, with such ease...she wouldn't soon forget it.

Maybe Oneiri Team really is done.

Without their leader, what were they? Could anyone replace Roach, and keep them unified as he had? Sure, both Jake and Ash had served briefly as commander, but Jake wasn't here, and she had serious doubts about her own ability to keep the team working together long-term.

Since graduation, Roach had wielded them like a single, seamless weapon.

Now, I feel like we're scattered.

"I wish we could go walk through the tall grass," Beth said, turning back as she spoke, her deep blue eyes shining.

"You're brave," Ash said, and she meant it. The real world really did feel less safe to her now, outside of the mech. "I don't have the courage to go outside the range of the snipers on the wall. Not anymore."

Wrinkling her cute little nose, Beth turned to continue walking. "It would be worth it, to feel the grass surrounding me. I think."

The wind picked up, and Ash caught a scent in the air she hadn't smelled in a while. "Hey," she called ahead. "Are you wearing perfume?"

"Yeah!" Beth said. "First time in months. And I don't know when I'll next get the opportunity, so..."

Ash smiled to herself. Her friend really did know how to make the best of every situation.

I wish I had that ability.

She wanted to help preserve her friend's good mood, but...

There are things we need to talk about.

"I'm concerned about Roach," she said at last. "I don't know that he can lead us anymore."

When Beth turned this time, the smile had vanished, and that killed Ash. "Seriously?" Beth said.

Ash nodded. "I mean, think about what he's become. What that thing he pilots did to him. He's basically an alien himself, now. Just a nervous system stretched across a metal frame."

Beth shuddered visibly.

"I wasn't going to mention this to anyone," Ash said. "Didn't want to worry them. But...the other day, he attacked me."

"What? How?"

"He hit me, sent me flying back inside my mech. I can send you the footage."

"No need—of course I believe you, Ash!"

"Yeah. I just thought you might want to see it."

"Well, you can send it if you want."

A silence fell between them, and it felt a bit awkward from Ash's perspective.

Oh, God. I've ruined a perfectly nice day. How many of those do we get?

An alert flashed on her HUD, then, with a high-enough priority that it superseded every other function of her implant.

"EMERGENCY BULLETIN: A FORCE CONSISTING OF FIFTY-THREE QUATRO AND THREE QUAD MECHS HAS BEGUN ATTACKING VILLAGES IN THE GLADES, TO THE SOUTHEAST OF INGRESS. ALL DARKSTREAM COMBAT UNITS ARE TO MUSTER AT INGRESS AND PREPARE FOR AN IMMINENT COUNTEROFFENSIVE."

After the implant detected that Ash had read the alert in full, it permitted her to will it to dissolve. When it did, her eyes found Beth's. "Did you get that alert?"

But by the way Beth's jaw was set, Ash could tell that she had. "I hate to say it, Steam," she said, "but we need Roach. We need *Dynamo.* We have to convince him to lead us again."

Ash nodded gravely. "You're right. But...I'll talk to him alone, okay?"

"Are you kidding me? After he attacked you? No way. I'm not letting you be alone with him."

"I have to, Paste. I have a trump card that I can use to persuade him, but it's not something I can share with anyone else. So it has to be just me. Okay?" Her last word sounded pleading, to Ash's own ears.

"Okay, Steam. But please be careful. I'll be nearby, and I'll be monitoring your status, to make sure you don't get into trouble. But I won't listen in."

"Thank you, Paste."

"Just be careful. I don't know what I'd do, if I lost...if I lost another teammate."

CHAPTER 12

A Unified Oneiri

"Chief Roach?" Ash said softly, almost whispering as she stopped several meters away from him, the memory of what he'd done during their last encounter fresh in her mind.

She'd gone to collect her **MIMAS** before braving this encounter—luckily, repairs on the mechs had just finished.

Roach was standing perfectly still outside the residence whose basement the quad had surfaced inside of. No one had yet made any effort to repair the gaping hole the Quatro had put in the structure's outer wall, leaving it instead for the elements to get inside and dampen the interior, creating an environment ideal for bacteria and mold.

"Sir?" Ash said, a little louder this time.

Roach didn't answer, or acknowledge her presence in any way.

Deciding to wait for a few moments, to see whether he was about to do anything rash, Ash's gaze drifted past him once more, to the wrecked home. From what she'd heard, the quadruped mech had killed the entire family that had resided there.

They'd gathered together for family dinner just before its arrival, and now they were all dead.

Had they been renting their house, or did they have a mortgage? *Maybe they owned it outright.* What would happen to it, now?

She wasn't sure why she was occupying herself with these thoughts as she waited for Roach to show some sign that there was still a human being somewhere inside the bulk of metal and weaponry he'd become.

Perhaps it was to remind herself of why they were fighting—not just to drive Darkstream profits, though that was certainly a big part of it; every employee knew that.

No, Darkstream doing well meant security for the system. That wasn't just PR; it was true. If she could help the company subdue the mounting alien threat, then she could create a safer planet for regular people to live on.

That's if Tessa Notaras's claims hold no water.

If what Tessa had said was true, then Darkstream was enslaving those regular people, and the line about providing them with system-wide security really was just a PR move, to placate the larger populations on Eresos and elsewhere.

Roach had called Notaras a liar. But the chief had also been exhibiting serious signs of mental instability, lately.

Ash sighed, and she accidentally transmitted it via the mech's broadcasting system.

That proved fortuitous, since it caused Roach to register her presence at last. He revolved in place, till his fearsome frame was squared with hers.

"*What?*" he said.

"Do you...do you still receive alerts from Darkstream, sir?"

"What are you here to discuss, Sweeney?"

"The rest of the team just received an emergency bulletin. Villages in the Glades are under attack by three quads and a whole bunch of Quatro."

"Then that's where I'm headed." Roach marched straight at her, fast, and she was forced to sidestep. His massive shoulder clipped hers as he passed, which made her mech whip around so that she was facing his receding back.

"You can't just go there by yourself, Dynamo," she called after him.

He kept striding forward, his pace totally unaltered.

"You need us," she said, yelling now. "You need Oneiri Team. Maybe you took out two quads, but your melding with that mech gave you an advantage in that fight." He still wasn't heeding her, so she jogged after him and continued shouting, even louder. "They know about that advantage now, and three quads working together to kill you will prove a much harder fighter than the two you caught off-guard. Not to mention the fifty-three Quatro not in mechs. We need a unified Oneiri Team to win this!"

Still nothing. Now, Roach began to run himself, and Ash could tell he was planning to rocket over the city walls again.

"You could die," she said. "And then you'll never avenge Jess."

That did it. The chief stopped, standing stock-still once more, facing away from her.

Ash stopped jogging, but she continued walking toward him. "I know that's why you were so hard on me in training. I know it's why you don't let yourself get too close to me, not even as close as teammates should get who have each other's backs. It's because I look just like her, isn't it? Every time you look at me, you see Jess, and it fills you with rage at your loss. That's why you were such an asshole to me last time we spoke. That's why you attacked me, even though I'm on your side—even though I've saved your life and you've saved mine."

She reached him, and she placed a metal hand on his shoulder, turning him gently but firmly. The fluid surface of his alien mech shimmered and shifted as he faced her, his inhuman face unreadable.

"It's why you're acting so irrationally—in a way that hurts your allies and hurts you. It also hurts your chances of avenging Jess. It's not fair to anyone, Chief. It's bull. And you can cut it out right now. Oneiri Team is going to that village together, and you're going to lead us there. Because you must."

A brittle silence stretched on. At last, Gabe spoke, and even though mediated by his mech, his voice was heavy with suppressed emotion: "Get the others together and meet me outside the city gates in thirty minutes. In thirty minutes, I'm leaving. I won't wait for another Darkstream battalion to gather, but if you want to follow me, you can. I've already abdicated my rank and position. But you can follow me. Don't ask for anything else, Sweeney, because it's all you're getting."

"Yes, *sir*," she said, and Roach jerked slightly, probably at her steadfast refusal to address him as anything except her military superior.

With that, she turned to jog down the street while switching to a team-wide channel.

CHAPTER 13

The Quatro Way

So it falls to me to try and clean up this mess, does it?

Lisa supposed that was fair. She had started this militia, and of its members, only she and Andy had recently been paid soldiers in the military Darkstream had established in the Steele System.

Andy was back with O'Toole and the Quatro drift they'd encountered, and anyway, he'd been a lower rank than her. Lisa had persuaded one of the Quatro to loan O'Toole a translator, so that he could communicate with his and Andy's hosts.

The bottom line was that Lisa was the de facto commander of this militia. Yes, Tessa had once ranked highly in Darkstream's military, but she had no interest in leading.

Which was good. Because the mess that Lisa had to clean up directly involved her.

In the short-term, the solution was fairly simple. She ordered Tessa to take another shuttle, while Rug remained in the one shared by Lisa, as well as Nail and Pen, the other Quatro who'd accompanied them from Alex, and Fan, which was the name chosen by the Quatro who'd left his drift to join them as their guide.

"You did not have to remove Tessa Notaras from my presence," Rug said, and if Lisa hadn't known better, she would have said the alien sounded sullen. "I would not have harmed her."

"You both need time apart from each other," Lisa said. "That's my judgment as commander, Rug." She wasn't accustomed to being so firm about her authority, but she knew it was necessary, especially since they were still figuring out the command structure of the militia. She sighed. "What you learned today...it's a lot to take in by itself, and it's a lot for your relationship with Tessa to bear. You need time apart, no matter what becomes of your friendship."

"If you say so," Rug said.

Of the nineteen Quatro who'd left Alex, four of them had decided not to accompany the militia on their journey to search for other Quatro drifts in the lands east of the Barrens. They'd been reunited with long-lost family, friends, and mates, and the temptation to remain behind with them had been great enough for them to abandon the cause.

Lisa didn't resent them for that, even though fewer Quatro accompanying them would probably mean lower chances of convincing the distant Quatro drifts to join their fight again Darkstream.

No, she didn't resent them. The opposite, actually: she admired them.

"Rug, I just want to say...I truly appreciate you and the others coming with us on this mission. Especially you. Your mate is still out there, clearly in trouble. Yet you're here, instead of looking for him."

"This is true," Rug said, swinging her head ponderously till her jet-black eyes met Lisa's. "But the needs of the drift must come before my own. You are one of my drift, Lisa. As is Tessa Notaras—even now."

Suppressing a grimace, Lisa decided she wanted to steer the conversation away from Tessa as much as she could. "A lot of the Quatro seem to be moving away from that sort of thinking," Lisa said. "Take the ones who stayed behind with family, even though their militia—their drift—needed them. Not saying I begrudge them that. I would have done the same, actually. But I *am* saying that a lot of your people appear to be stepping away from the drift-first mentality. They're finally putting themselves first."

Rug lay on the deck of the shuttle, though her head still rose just over Lisa's. Before, she'd looked fairly relaxed, but now she stiffened. "Your words contain a measure of truth. On Alex, my drift ceased reproduction due to the scarcity there, but with the resources the Eresos Quatro have, their population has likely multiplied by a factor of fifteen since their arrival."

"Whoa—Quatro reproduce that quickly?"

"Yes. Meaning the Quatro here are raising entire generations outside the Quatro way. But just because they are abandoning the ways of our people does not mean that I should."

Nodding, Lisa said, "Fair enough, I guess." A smile crept over her face. "Though I think you're going to change, too, Rug.

Stick around Steele System humans long enough, and we'll rub off on you."

The Quatro made a protracted snorting sound, similar to that which a horse might make. "I do not think it's wise to remain in the Steele System, for humans or for Quatro. You promised me you would bring us to our hidden ship in the Outer Ring. It is more than large enough to accommodate our militia. We must go there, Lisa Sato. You must keep your promise to us."

Lisa shifted in her crash seat, readjusting the straps. "I will," she muttered, then cleared her throat. "I will, Rug," she said, with more conviction. "It just can't be our main priority, right now. You understand that, don't you? Both our peoples are in terrible danger, here on Eresos. We have to stop Darkstream, and we have to figure out where all these strange mechs are coming from. From what I can tell, someone is trying to play both sides of this war. I just can't figure out why."

"I have figured it out already, Lisa, and I am happy to explain it to you. It is the Meddlers, doing what they have done before: meddle. They will return once the Gatherers fill their reservoirs with resources from the mines of Alex and Eresos—or rather, they'll come at the time they expect them the reservoirs to be filled. That is little more than a single year away, and when the Meddlers do come, there will be survival for few. Those that are left will be reduced to what my drift became, back on Alex: few in number, struggling to eke out a desperate existence."

Lisa sighed. "We'll get you to your ship, Rug."

"But will you get us to it in time? A year may not be enough for you to stop a war and initiate a mass exodus from this system."

"I haven't decided to leave this system, and neither have any other humans. We consider this our home, and we intend to stay here. We're prepared to defend it if we have to."

For a long time, Rug met her gaze while saying nothing.

Then, at last: "You do not grasp the incredible danger of the situation at hand, Lisa Sato. For that reason, I fear for us all."

CHAPTER 14

Without a
Spacefaring Enemy

Jake found it almost depressing, how lax security was aboard the *Javelin*. As a boy, his dreams of joining the military had been filled with soldiers who believed in self-discipline, strict protocol, and vigilance.

But without a spacefaring enemy to fight, the destroyer had turned into something that more closely resembled a floating resort for Bronson and his crew than it did a warship.

Sure, it still technically had military personnel, and despite the general sense of panic, they'd held their own in the battle against the alien machines.

Still.

The out-of-shape crewmembers. The Starlight Lounge. And now this...

The destroyer's main weapons locker, completely unguarded. Jake sighed as he strolled inside and began combing the racks for what he needed.

Tear gas...check. Flashbang grenades...check.

Fully loaded, fully automatic SL-17 assault rifle...check.

Though if this went well, he wouldn't have cause to use that. What he was planning already amounted to full-blown insubordination, of the sort that resulted in no mere slap on the wrist. Jake's punishment for what he was about to do would go well beyond demerits. It would mean a dishonorable discharge followed by a hefty fine and a lengthy jail sentence.

That was if they managed to apprehend him before he achieved his objective.

Before leaving, he loaded a pistol with a clip full of electric bullets, and he stowed a few more clips around his jumpsuit. He didn't want to hurt anyone—he just needed to make sure they couldn't stop him.

God help them if they try.

He opened the weapons locker hatch a crack, checking down the corridor before stepping into it and scanning the opposite direction. Nothing.

He progressed through several corridors that way, clutching his pistol with both hands, low but at the ready.

This is truly depressing. Even after the recent attack, the *Javelin*'s marines still weren't as on-alert as they should have been. The fact that there wasn't a single soldier within several corridors of the warship's primary weapons locker...

He repressed the urge to sigh again.

Checking around the next corner, he finally spotted some marines—a pair of them, ribbing each other about something, one of them holding a coffee in hand. They were both laughing loudly about whatever the subject of their fun was, so they didn't hear Jake's slow approach up the corridor.

They're about to feel real stupid.

He shot the one without a coffee in the neck, dropping him to the deck, a shuddering, jerking mess.

The other marine's mouth formed a comical "O" as she turned to register Jake's presence, her mug turning sideways to spill coffee onto the deck.

She, too, got an electric bullet in the neck.

The bullets were designed to continue delivering an electric shock over a prolonged period of time—enough to keep the target incapacitated but not enough to seriously injure them. The bullets were also meant to stop shocking the target well before permanent nerve damage was done.

Of course, no nonlethal weapon was perfect, and there were plenty of cases where things had gone wrong with the use of electric bullets.

Plenty of lawsuits against cops, back in the Milky Way.

That wouldn't be the consequence Jake faced if Darkstream apprehended him, however. He'd just be jailed and sucked dry of his personal finances.

But that would be far from the worst consequence of getting captured.

Far worse is the fact that my family would surely die.

He hated having to risk injuring his fellow soldiers, but this was what Bronson had driven him to. Maybe the Darkstream board of directors would have signed off on abandoning the innocent people of Hub to their fate—if that was the case, then they'd driven Jake to this, too.

Thinking you could stop me from protecting my family was your first mistake.

Jake cleared corridor after corridor. He'd planned all this out shortly after his conversation with Bronson. Briefly, he'd considered tying up his targets after stunning them with the electric bullets. Then, he'd realized that they would have sent out an alert using their implants the moment the shocks subsided. Until it did, they likely wouldn't have the concentration necessary to operate the implants, but that was all the time Jake had, unless he wanted to cut the damn implants out of the marines' heads.

So he moved swiftly, drawing closer and closer to the shuttle bay, taking as much care as he could afford to. Checking around each corner, moving from cover to cover. Neutralizing everyone he encountered.

Without warning, Captain Bronson himself emerged into an intersection of corridors ahead, turning the corner so that his back was to Jake. He held a coffee mug of his own.

"Captain," Jake barked.

Bronson turned around, and an expression of surprise had begun to blossom on his face when Jake shot him in the neck.

Pausing next to the captain's jerking form, Jake peered down at him, keeping his expression neutral. "I didn't want to shoot you while you weren't looking at me."

Within five minutes, he reached the shuttle bay. Lowering his faceplate, he turned on his jumpsuit's life support before using his S-level security clearance to open the hatch.

Good thing I still have that clearance. It served as further evidence that he'd caught the crew of the *Javelin* with their pants down.

Across the shuttle bay, four marines surrounded the alien mech, which wasn't unusual—Bronson had ordered a rotating guard of four soldiers shortly after the mech had been brought aboard, though Jake wasn't sure what good they would do if the thing activated and started to attack.

That posed the biggest danger in all of this: whether the alien mech would accept him inside it, or whether it would kill him. It was a risk he had to take, however. The thing clearly had the ability to operate in space, and if it was anything like the smaller robots that had almost succeeded in dismantling the destroyer, it could do so for long periods. If those robots *hadn't* had that ability, they would never have attempted to make the journey to the inner system, to Eresos, which Bronson had told him they had.

Unclipping a flashbang from his belt, Jake hurled it across the shuttle bay in a broad parabola.

His aim was good. The flashbang landed between the two marines closest to him, who seemed roughly as oblivious as those he'd encountered in the corridors.

One of them glanced down at it—just before it went off, sending both marines reeling, hands clamped to their ears, eyes squeezed shut.

The pair of marines on the far side of the alien mech rushed around it, but Jake was already sprinting across the shuttle bay for a better shot. He dispatched one of them with an electric bullet to the neck, and the next with one to the cheek.

Whoops. He hadn't meant to hit anyone in the face, and he hoped it wouldn't result in too much scarring.

"Thank Bronson for that, not me," Jake said as he stepped over the marine's writhing body in order to get to the alien mech. He said it more for himself than for the marine, he knew. He was still trying to convince himself that he was doing the right thing.

After the flurry of action his rush from the weapons locker to the shuttle bay had required, it felt odd to stand there and stare up at the mech's alien face. The thing would still be disabled from the EMP he'd hit it with outside the destroyer, and this part of Jake's plan involved effecting some hasty repairs. He'd been taught to perform mech repairs during training on Valhalla, before ever deploying to Eresos, but he hadn't been trained to do them under the time constraints he now faced.

Plus, I learned to repair a MIMAS mech, not an alien one.

"Stop right there!" a stern voice barked.

Jake whirled around, raising his pistol to point toward the hatch. There, he saw the woman who'd yelled at him. She stood at the head of a squad of marines, all with guns trained on Jake.

He cursed under his breath. *So I get no time to do repairs, then.*

To confront so many enemies at this range, his pistol was useless. He dropped it to the deck, grasping his SL-17 where it was slung by his right side.

With his left hand, he grabbed one of the jerking marines by the back of his jumpsuit, taking care not to come in contact with the man's skin to avoid getting shocked. Jake pulled the solider up until the assault rifle's muzzle met the back of his head.

"Shoot and you spend this man's life," Jake yelled, his voice wavering a little. He hadn't expected it to come to this—he didn't see himself as the sort of person who *did* this. "All I'm trying to do is leave without hurting anyone. I don't know if you've heard, but Hub is under attack. That's where my family lives. Bronson's already informed me he has no intention of going there to help, so I'm taking matters into my own hands. I hope any of you would do the same."

The woman opened her mouth as if to answer, but no words came out.

Jake glanced at the alien construct. "Are you going to let me inside, mech?" It felt completely absurd to address the thing, especially since he knew it was still disabled, but what else was there? Attempting to repair the mech would be impossible while clutching his hostage, with ten marines pointing weapons at him.

Incredibly, the mech opened—from the front, which Jake hadn't seen before. A hatch fell forward to *clang* to the floor, forming a convenient ramp for Jake to ascend.

Clearly, the mech had taken it upon itself to repair the damage from the EMP, which should not have been possible.

Obviously it is possible, though. So...it's just been sitting here all this time, fully functional? Waiting for...what? Me?

That sent shivers up Jake's spine, but he had no choice except to take advantage of the mech's unexpected functionality. He ascended the ramp backward, dragging the marine up with him. Jake's eyes never left the marines near the shuttle bay's hatch.

Once he was seated inside the alien mech, he jettisoned the marine, and the man crashed to the floor, still shaking from the electric bullet lodged in his neck. Jake immediately popped a fast-acting, REM sleep-inducing sedative into his mouth.

The mech sealed up instantly, the ramp snapping up to become one with the rest.

Jake entered the mech dream, and as he looked out on the shuttle bay with the mech's eyes, a terrible anxiety took root deep inside him.

Doing his best to ignore it, he strode toward the airlock, willing his hands to become ultra-thin wedges. He drove those into the crack between the doors and wrenched them open enough to grip them with fingers that reformed in an instant.

He closed the inner door behind him and then pulled open the outer one. That done, he blasted out of the airlock and into the void.

CHAPTER 15

Sabotage

It was Lisa's shift to monitor the pilot and make sure he wasn't doing anything to sabotage their mission.

They no longer kept a weapon trained directly at his head—that seemed like overdoing it, at this point. The man seemed compliant enough.

That said, he remained a Darkstream employee, and Lisa still wondered how much of a loyalist he was. Would his affection for his employer lead him to put himself in danger for the company? Or was that above his pay grade?

Best not to take any chances.

Lisa's hand did not stray very far from the pistol holstered near her hip. She'd adjusted it for easy access, even as she reclined in the copilot's seat, which rarely got used outside of training. The shuttle's AI was typically copilot enough.

The pilot had devoted most of the cockpit's screens to views of the terrain below, and Lisa found it hard not to get distracted by the landscape as it gradually transformed, from rolling forests filled with leafless trees to a craggy, uneven desert region.

Recently, she'd read on the system net that Darkstream was planning to start switching all their vehicles to an interface similar to the one Oneiri Team used to control their mechs. All new vehicles would be built with it from the get-go, and existing ones would be retrofitted.

According to the post she'd read, the company seemed pretty adamant that within two years, every employee that drove or piloted a Darkstream vehicle would feel like they *were* that vehicle, be it a beetle, speeder, shuttle, warship, or mech. As with the mechs, they felt it would increase immersion while granting pilots a proper respect for their mechanical charges.

Lisa wasn't sure how she felt about it. Her training with Tessa had left her with serious misgivings about the actual utility of lucid, and the idea of turning warfare into one big dream didn't sit all that well with her.

Real people died in war, and real lives were ruined. That cost was steep enough, but to inflict it while you were actually *asleep...*

Doesn't seem great.

Andy, on the other hand, would probably love it. Anything that gave him greater control of his beetle, or whatever else he ended up driving—Lisa felt sure that would be all fine by him.

Something on one of the viewscreens caught her eye. "Hold up," she barked, and the pilot stiffened. "What is that? Zoom in on that region, there." Lisa pointed at one of the screens, and the pilot winced when her finger touched the display.

"If you could refrain from actually touching the monitors—"

"Shut up and zoom in!"

This time, he listened. And when the view magnified, Lisa beheld what appeared to be a parade of Gatherers. There were more than she'd ever seen in one place.

"That has to be a sign of *someone* living nearby," she muttered. *Hopefully, it's the new Quatro friends we hope to make.* "Take us down. But before you do," Lisa said, raising her voice, and holding her index finger an inch from the pilot's face, "check the region thoroughly for Amblers. You'll be coming with us as we search this area, so if you try to send us into danger, you'll be there too, to endure it with us."

"I understand," the pilot said, his voice flat.

"Good."

CHAPTER 16

Blaring Prophecy

The alien mech dream was not like the one he'd used to interface with his MIMAS.

Inside this one, everything had a stark, dire quality to it. Sounds were crisper—or at least, they'd been back in the shuttle bay, before he'd entered the soundless void of space—and sights were more vivid, but not in a way that was beautiful or calming. Instead, it was as though he viewed the universe through a filter that accentuated the essential tension that underlaid everything. Wasn't every last particle just a blaring prophecy of the death that awaited every living thing? Someday, everyone he'd ever known or loved would cease to be, their carbon dispersing into the void, conserved in a sense but not in a sense that meant anything.

Why didn't I ever think about that, before? Why wasn't it foremost in my mind, every second of every single day?

It felt incredibly irresponsible that he hadn't constantly dwelled on it, now. Maybe, if he had, his family wouldn't be in the danger they were currently in.

It's possible they're already dead. Have you considered that?

Of course he'd considered it. But he didn't dare think about it.

Other than the fact that it was all he could think about.

Something collided with his face—the mech's face—clinging to the metal skin, rending it with tiny claws. Within seconds, scraps of Jake's face floated through the void, streaming behind him, and that caused him alarm. He aimed his jets forward, to arrest his momentum, to try and reclaim the pieces of his face.

Oh. Probably he should deal with the little creature trying to penetrate the mech and access his flesh-and-blood body, as well.

He reached up and plucked it off, which cleared his vision sensors. The moment he did, he recalled that he could probably patch through the feed from anywhere in his body, just as he had in his **MIMAS**.

He held his attacker in front of his face, studying it. It was a robot identical to those that had attacked the *Javelin* and then headed for Eresos, and it writhed in his grasp, trying to free it-self.

It wouldn't have stood much chance of doing that even if Jake had still been piloting his **MIMAS**, but in the alien mech's grip, its probability of escape was exactly zero.

He'd used his **MIMAS** to tear one of the robots in two, but now he simply clenched his fist, and the robot fragmented.

We should call them Ravagers. It suits their behavioral pat-terns.

"Wait," Jake muttered. "We?"

His thoughts had already seemed detached, from both reality and from himself, but he'd chalked that up to the fundamental strangeness of this new mech dream.

Now, he began to wonder whether those thoughts had a source outside himself. *Either that, or I'm going crazy.*

That thought had been his. He felt pretty sure of it.

Pretty sure.

"Ravager is a good name, though." He thrust backward gently, and as he did, the shreds of his face reunited with his body, to become part of his shoulders and neck.

Another Ravager crashed into Jake's back, sending him forward.

Acting solely on instinct, Jake *inverted,* so that his feet pointed in the opposite direction, along with his face. His arms and legs and torso all switched around so that he about-faced without actually turning.

That done, he plucked the Ravager from his new chest and crushed it.

That's two, now.

Far behind him—ahead of him, now, rather—something gleamed dully in the dim sunlight that reached this far into the outer system.

Is that another—?

A third Ravager charged into him from his right, making him jolt to the left, and a fourth and fifth collided with his lower back, while a sixth landed on his head.

His four new visitors started to tear at the surface of his mech right away. Three more impacts followed, jerking the alien mech this way and that in the inertia-less void. Then five more impacts, all in quick succession.

I need to act.

And he did act, tearing the Ravagers from his body as fast he could manage it, all while the remaining creatures burrowed deeper, inching closer to the cocoon where Jake's unconscious form was nestled.

More of them arrived, hitting him with various degrees of force. One connected with such speed that it sent Jake hurtling backward, end over end, and though there was no gravity the sight of the system's ecliptic plane spinning so frenetically made him feel nauseated, even inside the dream.

This mech dream had new ways of communicating negative emotions—of maintaining his immersion in the battle and of communicating the danger he was in. The temperature seemed to skyrocket, and he felt like he was cooking. A minor note began to play: an eerie, one-note ballad performed by a violin in need of tuning. The volume ratcheted up quickly.

His fear and rage reached a crescendo, and his fight-or-flight instinct took over.

Until he did it, he hadn't known what he was about to do:

Jake exploded.

Jagged spires erupted all over his metal skin; one for each Ravager.

Most of the smaller robots ruptured, sending dozens of fragments sailing through the void in dozens of directions, but a few of them stayed intact enough to remain impaled on the tips of the spires.

The spires slowly retracted into him, although Jake wasn't sure he'd willed them to. He wasn't sure he'd willed them to emerge in the first place.

Could it have been my subconscious?

He didn't know. At any rate, no more Ravagers attacked. Either that had been the last of them, or the feat he'd just performed had scared them into full retreat.

Trying to still his racing heart, and to lower the furnace the dream had continued to simulate, Jake continued his voyage through the Belt, toward Hub.

He was attacked again by Ravagers less than ten minutes later. They quickly covered him, making alarming progress in their efforts to infiltrate the mech and rip Jake from it bodily.

At first, he couldn't replicate the trick with the spires. But when his aggravation peaked, it happened once more, destroying his enemies in one fell swoop.

Ten minutes later, they attacked again.

Bronson had said that clouds of the robots had set a course for Eresos, but here more were, out in the Belt. With that in mind, as well as the attack on Hub, Jake realized that something fundamental had changed. Not just for the Belt, but for the entire Steele System.

It wasn't safe here, anymore. And based on Bronson's actions, the only military in the system was no longer devoted to the safety of the population.

If it had ever been.

CHAPTER 17

Avalanche

L isa wiped a bead of sweat from her brow as she pulled herself up yet another sharp rise.

Navigating is brutal, here.

A few meters to her left, Rug easily stepped onto the rise, pulling herself up with her front paws. The rise was even steeper where she climbed it.

Helps to be a giant alien, I guess.

Fan, the Quatro acting as their guide on the journey to find the distant drifts, had said those drifts were "across the Barrens." That had made Lisa expect a dramatic change in scenery—from desert to jungle, maybe, or lush wetlands.

But they'd flown a long way in the shuttles, and so far the terrain seemed basically indistinguishable from the Barrens. It was just as dry, just as uneven, and just as treacherous.

Andy probably would have made fun of her for not knowing much about Eresos' geography and what to expect from it. But these lands reminded her of Alex's landscape, and as they followed the Gatherers through them, she wished for a beetle.

The only reason she didn't order a return to the shuttles was the fact that the Gatherers were clearly heading somewhere with purpose. And if they could make it wherever they were going, then so could whoever lived there, and so could the soldiers of Lisa's militia.

"Careful, Vickers," she called ahead. "Take that corner carefully."

"Yes, ma'am." Rodney Vickers was on point, and currently he was about to enter a ravine with steep, dusty-brown walls.

He crept forward, rocket launcher at the ready, and quickly scrambled back, falling on his backside as heavy machine gun fire tore up the ground where he'd been standing. The shoulder-fired rocket launcher fell to the ground with a wince-inducing *crack*.

"It's an Ambler, ma'am, headed toward us!"

Lisa cursed. "Everyone, full retreat, now! Double-time!"

Exchanging glances with Tessa, she could tell the other woman grasped the situation just as well as she did, which wasn't a surprise.

They'd just finished crossing a craggy, open expanse, which had been treacherous to traverse but which offered inconsistent cover.

There was no way they could take out the Ambler, not without losing most of the militia. She'd only heard reports of two ever being taken down in the history of Eresos—one by three full platoons of Darkstream soldiers, and another by Quatro, which had resulted in dozens of them dead.

There was a good chance that, if they tried to take one on here, they could all die.

That meant...

"We need to stay and hold it off if we can," Lisa said. "Try to give the others time to cross that open terrain." Just before the expanse, there'd been another ravine, narrower than the one ahead, which the Ambler would not be able to chase them through.

But traveling back to it is another matter altogether.

It had taken them ten minutes to cross the open region, while taking their time, and it would take at least five to do so again at a run—providing no one suffered any injuries.

"We have other problems," Tessa said, pointing.

Lisa followed the gesture to a cliff face on her left—which their shuttle pilot was in the process of scaling.

"Incredible," she muttered, then turned back to Tessa, eyebrows raised. "You got that?"

"I can shoot him down." Tessa hefted her assault rifle. "Making the shot from here will be easy."

"Tessa, will you cut it out?" Ever since Rug had learned about her past, Tessa's unflinching bravery had turned into a recklessness that had Lisa constantly on edge. "There's no way we'd get him across that terrain with a bullet wound. We sort of need him."

The white-haired woman scowled, lowering her SL-17. Then she raised it again and shot the cliff just above the pilot, raining dirt and rock fragments down on his head. "Any higher and I'll shoot you off that rock!" she yelled.

"You'll never do it!" the Darkstream pilot shouted back. "You need me!" He kept climbing.

"Damn it," Tessa spat, tossing her gun onto the ground.

"You need to climb up after him," Lisa said, her words clipped.

For several long seconds, the older woman held her gaze, her face hard. Finally, she muttered, "Yes, *ma'am,*" and jogged stiffly toward the cliff.

Most of the militia had followed Lisa's order to fall back across the open terrain, but Rug remained, as well as Rodney Vickers.

The Quatro stepped forward. "I will help you protect the others, Lisa Sato."

Nodding, Lisa said, "Thank you, Rug." Her gaze drifted up to the alien's shoulders, where her energy weapons were still mounted.

"Can you use those things in this heat?" she asked. The Quatro lacked hands, but their brains were laced with super-conducting fullerenes, allowing them to manipulate metals. Their power weakened dramatically as the temperature rose, however.

"I have turned down the pressure required to depress the trigger to the minimum setting possible," Rug said. "I do not know for certain, as I've never attempted to operate them in this level of heat. But I will try."

"Okay." If Rug could make the weapon work, it could actually make a difference in holding off the Ambler. It would be the first time she knew of that energy guns had ever been used on one.

"It's coming!" Vickers said.

Lisa looked. The Ambler was indeed stalking into view, swiveling, no doubt seeking its prey.

"Get back down to the lower level!" she yelled, scrambling back over the rise she'd recently climbed. The others followed. Rug had to crouch quite low to the ground to avoid exposing any part of her to the Ambler's weapons.

Lisa could hear it as the giant mech strode toward them, sending a tremor through the ground with every step.

"Give me that," Lisa said, nodding at the militia's only rocket launcher, which Vickers had insisted on carrying from the shuttles.

The man frowned. "But..."

"Give it to me, Vickers. Now!"

Reluctantly, he handed it over, and Lisa gave him her SL-17. That done, she inspected the rocket launcher and saw that it seemed intact, even after Vickers had dropped it in his panic to escape the Ambler.

"Okay," she said. "Here's the plan. Rug, you pop up and distract the Ambler with your energy gun. Fire, duck, change your location, and repeat. Vickers, you fire on it if Rug is taking too much heat, and switch up your location, too."

"What will you do?" Vickers said.

"The Ambler's sticking close to the cliff on our left, and the way that cliff tapers outward at the top looks pretty unstable.

I'm going to see if I can dislodge anything with a rocket, send it down on the Ambler's head. Got it?"

"Got it!" Vickers said.

"I understand," Rug said.

"Then go. Both of you!"

They spread out, firing on the Ambler from spots far enough away that Lisa wouldn't get hit by errant shots from the mech.

Looks like Rug's gun is working after all. Thank God.

But she couldn't execute her part of the plan just yet.

She opened a two-way channel between her and Tessa. "Tessa, report!"

"He made it up the cliff, but I caught up to him. It's pretty flat up here, so if you can make it back to the shuttles, you should be able to land one here to pick us up."

A wave of relief washed over Lisa. "Excellent. How far away from the cliff are you?"

"He made it twenty meters before I caught up to him."

"Drag him farther away from it, if you can. Sato out."

She waited for Rug to unleash her next energy barrage, and when she did, Lisa popped up over the rise and scanned the cliff above the Ambler.

As she'd hoped, the energy weapon was doing some damage to the great war machine. It recoiled a little with each shot, and much of its front was singed from the hits it had already taken.

It staggered backward as Rug hit it again—right underneath a boulder that loomed overhead.

Lisa lined up the launcher and took her shot, aiming for the cliff just under the boulder and praying for it to collapse.

It did. The large rock tumbled down, connecting with the Ambler's giant dome of a head and sending it stumbling into the open.

That was good, but the Ambler was far from finished, and now it had moved away from the cliff. As promising as Rug's success with the energy weapon was, Lisa knew it couldn't neutralize the enemy robot by itself.

"Rug, we need to drive it back to the cliff!"

"I am trying," the Quatro shouted. "However, whenever I fire on it, the return fire forces me to stop. I need a bigger window."

Racking her brain for a solution, Lisa glanced at Vickers. Then she shoved the launcher at him.

He accepted it, eyes gleaming. The assault rifle clattered to the hard ground, and Lisa picked it up.

"I'm going out there," she said. "To distract it, and to take some pressure off Rug. She'll use the opening to force the Ambler back against the cliff, and when she does, I need you to make it collapse on top of it. Think you can do that?"

"I was born to do that," Vickers said, sounding breathless.

"Good." She raised her voice. "Rug, you're about to get your window!"

Lisa moved.

The Ambler seemed to notice her the moment she appeared above the rise, and it swiveled to turn autocannons on her.

Sprinting as hard as she could, Lisa felt shrapnel biting into her ankles as the enemy tore up the ground directly behind her.

I need to keep moving. If she didn't, the Ambler would have the opportunity to cook her with its lasers. *If it doesn't decide to simply rip me apart with its autocannons.*

"Rug!" she yelled, and it was all she had the breath for.

At last, the energy weapon started firing, and the Ambler was not in position to return fire. Instead, it sent random shots zipping through the air over Lisa's head, and she fell into a prone position, scrambling to turn herself around and fire on the mech.

Her SL-17 probably didn't contribute much, but the energy weapon was doing enough work for the both of them. The Ambler fell back, still trying to reorient itself to fire back at its tormentors.

Then, Vickers' rocket hit, and it did exactly what Lisa had hoped. The top of the cliff gave way, sending a cascade of dirt and boulders crashing down onto the Ambler.

A particularly large boulder connected with its head, denting it and causing the massive machine to collapse. The avalanche soon blocked it from view.

"This is the best chance we'll get!" Lisa screamed over the tumult. "Move, you two. *Move!*"

They turned to flee over the uneven terrain as fast as they could. Behind them, Lisa was sure she heard the pile of rocks shifting as the Ambler struggled to regain its feet.

CHAPTER 18

The Glades

He really needs to slow down. This is getting ridiculous.

In the thirty minutes Roach had given her to gather Oneiri Team, Ash had tried to get some additional Darkstream forces together for the mission to the Glades.

She'd failed, though, and it wouldn't have mattered either way. The moment the five remaining **MIMAS** mechs of Oneiri Team gathered together outside the city gates, Chief Roach took off without another word, pounding across the grassy plains—far too fast for any ground unit that wasn't a mech to keep up.

He'd barely altered his pace at all since then, and at some point Ash realized that he meant to reach the Glades today, and probably to engage the Quatro if he could find them before nightfall.

It took everything Ash had to keep up with Roach as they pounded through dense woods, dodging around massive trees, leaping over jagged stumps.

Even though it was the **MIMAS** that actually endured the strain of running this fast for this long, the mech dream translated the exertion into a visceral experience, so that it felt like she was the one whose endurance was being taxed.

It amounted to the same thing. With every mile, it became harder and harder to continue the breakneck pace, and it took just as much will for her to continue running as it would have if she'd been running in her own body.

In the meantime, her implant helpfully informed her that she hadn't eaten since the modest breakfast she'd had early that morning.

Now, dusk lengthened shadows across Eresos' surface, and her body needed nourishment. She'd be fine without it, but if Roach had been looking out for the wellbeing of his team he would have ordered a stop.

"What's wrong with him?" Beth subvocalized over a two-way with Ash, and she could hear the tension in Paste's voice—from the simulated exertion, no doubt, but probably also from the anxiety that stemmed from not knowing what Roach was planning. Ash certainly felt that, herself.

"I don't know," she rasped back. "He's not the same as he was."

"Think it's something to do with that thing he lives inside, now?"

Ash considered that for a moment. "Not sure. He seemed to change even before that. When he came back half-dead from chasing that quad...his behavior worried me back then. Now, though...I don't know. He's different, for sure, no matter what's causing it."

"He needs to get his shit together. We're counting on him. Everyone is."

"I'm not sure he cares. About anything, other than killing Quatro."

"Well, we have that in common."

Ahead, the woods began to thin—a telltale sign of an upcoming glade, for which this region had taken its name. Not all the glades had villages, but this one did, according to Ash's HUD.

Indeed, she soon spotted the first structure. And then the next.

Something struck her as odd, and at first, she couldn't quite put her finger on it. Then, she had it:

There aren't any lights on. It's getting too late to get around unassisted. And not everyone would be inside. Not on a night like this.

Of course, a bulletin about Quatro in the area would have gone out to every village, and maybe this one had blacked out intentionally, to avoid attracting attention.

That makes sense. Still, an eerie feeling dogged her as they began to pass the first houses.

She used her S-level security clearance to access Darkstream's database of implants and v-lenses. The company made and sold the devices everyone used to access the system net, and they took the liberty of tracking each one's location, which was a fact known only to certain operatives.

If you had the knowhow, you could disable that 'feature,' but most people didn't even know it existed in the first place, even though the fact of it was buried somewhere inside the End User

License Agreement. The clause had even been published on the system net, but not many people spent their time on the system net reading articles about privacy and security issues.

When Ash consulted the database, she could find no indication that any v-lens or implant was active inside the entire village.

"It's deserted," Ash said.

Marco nodded in confirmation. Knowing him, he'd probably done the same thing she had.

Roach had stopped in the center of the village green, and now he revolved slowly, taking in the structures surrounding them.

From the way the other MIMAS mechs twitched, Ash could tell that they found Roach's behavior just as creepy as she did.

A *cracking* came from Ash's right, and she whirled just in time to see the quad that was crashing out of the building two meters away from her, eyes glowing bright red in the dark.

It charged, knocking her backward onto the ground while it sank lengthening claws into her mech's shoulder.

The night sky flashed scarlet.

CHAPTER 19

Comet Four

Using the alien mech's thrusters, Jake was capable of rapid acceleration—much faster than the comet hoppers—and in the void of space, there was nothing to impede that acceleration, other than the comets of the Belt. As long as he succeeded in avoiding those, he could pile speed on top of incredible speed.

Jake might have accelerated indefinitely, reaching Hub in astonishing time—if he'd had unlimited fuel. The alien mech was a technological wonder, and the dream had already highlighted comets as an excellent source of hydrogen fuel.

He availed of that, of course, but it did entail stopping, and after each refueling he needed to begin his acceleration all over again.

The Ravager attacks did not help matters, though they grew less frequent as he neared Hub.

That worried him, since it probably meant that any Ravagers in the neighborhood had been diverted to the effort to take out the only major settlement the Belt had.

Someone's intent on scrubbing humanity from this system quickly.

But who? And why wasn't Bronson more concerned? If he'd been Bronson, he would have prioritized the defense of Hub.

Losing it would represent a huge blow, strategically, since this was the system's only presence out here. On the other hand, repelling the attackers would send a message that humanity was not to be trifled with.

Bronson has to listen to the board, I guess. But that didn't mean Jake forgave the man for abandoning the people of Hub, and for ordering Jake to do the same.

At last, Hub came into view: seven large comets, all roughly the same size, and all connected to a central control center using super-strong nanotethers that were tens of thousands of kilometers long.

Hub's design allowed for the addition of more comets without upsetting the structure's rotation, and it allowed for their subtraction as well. In the event that something went catastrophically wrong with one comet, the other six would continue to spin, unaffected.

The comets averaged around a mile and a half in diameter. Residents used small craft to visit their neighbor comets, whether for business or pleasure. Each comet had a single landing bay, all of which faced inward—a testament to the fact that the inhabitants considered theirs to be a community cloistered from the rest of the universe.

And it pretty much is.

Except, now it was overrun by Ravagers—the peaceful paradise compromised, possibly ruined forever. Hub's inhabitants had stopped posting updates of their plight shortly after the post Jake had read. He'd tried sending several messages, to his family, to old neighbors, to members of the Council, and to everyone else he could think of.

No one had responded.

Maybe I'm too late. Maybe everyone was already dead.

But he wasn't prepared to entertain that thought. Not yet. Jake had designed his entire life around keeping his sister alive, and the idea that she might have been murdered by an alien robot instead of the carcinoma that they'd all been battling together for years...

He tried contacting his mother once again, and even though he was within real-time communications range now, Brianne Price still didn't answer.

So he headed for the second-largest of the seven comets that formed Hub. It was called Comet Four, and it was also where he'd grown up.

When he jetted to the outer airlock, which was big enough to admit the old combat shuttles Bronson and the other rogue UHF captains had brought with them when they first fled to the Steele System, he found the hatch smashed open.

The minor violin note returned, from when he'd fought the Ravagers en route to here. This time, that was the only way the mech dream chose to represent his distress.

As though he needed an external indicator of the potent mix of shock and fear that raged within him.

The emergency backup hatch failed to engage.

In the event of a breach, the landing bay was supposed to enter Lockdown Mode, to prevent the comet's atmosphere from escaping into space.

But it hadn't. Instead, it had been expelled from the comet where Jake's family lived in a great rush.

No one could have survived that.

Not unless they'd had advance warning of the attack, of course. There were emergency shelters, installed for exactly such an eventuality, and if you made it to them in time, you could make it. They were kept oxygenated, pressurized, and well-stocked with food and supplies.

At least, they're supposed to be.

If his home comet had not been the first one attacked, it was possible his family had had enough advance notice to make it to a shelter. Doing that with all of the equipment and medicine necessary to keep Sue Anne alive would have made that tedious, but it was possible.

A slim hope. But a hope nonetheless.

Jake jetted past the airlock and through the shuttle bay. The inner airlock was clogged up with everything from the comet that hadn't been secured—a miscellany consisting of wooden boards, tools, speeders, and even the mangled corpses of livestock. The buildup didn't create a perfect seal, though. Jake could see light shining through the barrier, meaning it wouldn't have acted to preserve any of the comet's oxygen.

He rocketed through the plug, flinging its contents every which way before the various objects hurtled once more toward the airlock, many of them continuing through to the landing bay before the barrier recreated itself.

Only as he'd crashed through had Jake realized that some of the corpses were human.

He tried to put the revelation out of his mind, and as he entered the comet, the Ocharium nanites inside his cells engaged with the Majorana fermions buried beneath the ground, which resulted in a simulated one G.

Of course, it shouldn't have been that easy, given the giant alien mech that he piloted. But it was—the mech behaved as though it was subjected to one G, as well.

Does it contain Ocharium too? Or has it synced with my body's experience of simulated gravity using some other method?

He didn't know, and right now he had no time to puzzle over it.

Peering around his childhood home did nothing to alleviate his mounting anxiety. The central, artificial sun still lit everything as brightly as it always had, from its perch atop the thin spire that stretched up three-quarters of a mile. The 'sun' rested in the very center of the comet, and if anything had gone wrong with it, there would have been much bigger problems. A thermonuclear reactor powered it.

Jake could see basically everything in the comet from where he stood, which was true of anywhere you cared to stand inside it. The land curved up and away from him, and residences hung directly overhead, too—as well as copses of trees and lush, green fields.

At least, they'd once been lush. The tiny woods had mostly been burned, and many of the fields were scorched, too. Jake was sure the vegetation had lost much of its original color, also—probably because of the oxygen being vented out of the comet.

Ravagers crawled all over, wreaking destruction wherever they could.

And when his eyes fell on his family's house, he saw that it had been blasted apart, with only charred ruins left of his childhood home.

CHAPTER 20

Whirlwind of Metal

Ash tried to buck off her assailant, but the quad was far too heavy, and with it pinning her she couldn't bring any of her weapons to bear.

The Quatro mech's claws dug deep into the circuitry and servomotors of Ash's shoulder, causing the dream to go berserk, in a way she'd never seen it do before.

As two more *cracking* sounds signaled more quads breaking out of structures, one of her fellow MIMAS pilots rocketed into the one pinning her down.

The thing seemed to be ready for the maneuver, and it only shifted a meter before producing spikes to fire from its shoulders, straight at the MIMAS that had helped Ash, which her HUD said was piloted by Henrietta Jin.

Henrietta extended both her bayonets, knocking the spikes aside before they hit her. With that, she used her right bayonet to parry a swipe from one of the quad's mighty paws before thrusting forward with her left, putting her weight behind it.

The blade plunged into the enemy's metal chest, the fluid metal surface seeming to peel back in alarm before attempting to expel the bayonet. But Henrietta took a step forward, sinking her blade farther in.

By now, Ash had regained her feet, and she circled around to the right, training her lasers on the alien's flank.

The quad writhed, seeming to panic, and Ash brought all her focus to bear, making sure she kept the beams on that one spot.

Something hit her from behind, knocking her forward, and then the quad managed to wrench away from Henrietta's assault, turning tail and fleeing.

Extending her bayonets, Ash whipped around savagely, swiping at whatever had attacked her with the sharp edge.

Her blade found a Quatro neck, and she followed through, parting it from the alien's shoulders. The massive, headless body slumped to the ground.

I got lucky with that one.

But more Quatro rushed in between the buildings, and Oneiri was instantly surrounded by the massive aliens, who crashed against them like a purple tide.

"They were waiting to ambush us!" Ash grunted as she dropped to one knee, turning a Quatro's charge against it by sending it up and over her. She surged upward, and though the effort felt clumsy and awkward, it messed up the Quatro's landing. That gave Ash time to detach her heavy machine gun from her back and riddle the alien with bullets.

"Typical Quatro behavior," Henrietta said. She hadn't retracted her bayonets yet, choosing instead to plunge them repeatedly into whatever Quatro deigned to come at her.

"The good news is, I think we have your nickname," Ash said as she continued to shoot the Quatro she'd tossed. It was now staggering toward her.

"Oh God. This should be good."

"Razor. For the way you shave these Quatro so good!"

Henrietta chuckled. "It's actually not bad."

Another Quatro leapt at Ash, knocking her gun sideways, and if she hadn't stopped firing instantly she would have hit Henrietta.

Incensed, Ash sent a metal fist into the Quatro's face, causing blood to spray. It reared back, shaking its head, and she jammed the heavy machine gun in its face, pulling the trigger.

The beast's head exploded, sending brain and viscera to splatter against Ash's metal skin.

Two down. She searched for her next target.

It didn't take her very long to find one. Most of the other mechs were faring much worse than she was. She couldn't see Richaud and Beth, but a massive pile of writhing Quatro gave her a good idea of where they might be.

Firing a couple grenades into that dogpile, she moved to lend Spirit a hand, mowing down a Quatro before it could complete its headlong charge into his backside.

He was engaged with two other foes, and didn't seem to notice the assist. *I never get any credit,* Ash reflected sardonically, shifting the gun toward her next target.

Then, she saw Chief Roach, and she quickly realized that as hard as the rest of Oneiri Team had it, they were playing on easy mode.

Roach was taking on three quads at once—and he was winning.

A whirlwind of metal and ordnance, Roach sent fragment after fragment of himself hurtling toward his opponents, whose measured movements spoke of respect for their adversary.

Ash began to turn to see whether she could help the mechs pinned underneath the Quatro, but before she could, she witnessed one of the quads foolishly charge at Roach, in a desperate attempt to run him through with the lance that sprouted from its chest as it ran.

It succeeded in impaling him, right where Roach would have been—if he'd still had a human body.

As it was, the attack only gave him the proximity he needed to swing two newly morphed scythes down at the quad.

Both blades sank deep into the quadruped mech, and when Roach removed them, it fell lifelessly to the ground.

One of the remaining quads let out a strange sound, which resembled a cross between a roar and a smoker's cough.

The rest of the Quatro instantly extracted themselves from the battle with Oneiri, following the two quads Roach hadn't killed yet as they fled the village.

"To me!" Roach called, and a thrill shot through Ash—at their sudden victory but also at the fact that Roach was acknowledging that he needed them. That they functioned best as a team.

"They'll attack other villages if we let them escape," he went on. "We must run them down."

As the Quatro fled, Roach took aim at one of their backsides with arms that rapidly became energy cannons.

Blue light lanced forward, and the rear third of a Quatro simply incinerated.

"*Move!*" Roach screamed, and they did.

CHAPTER 21

The Gatherers

They'd almost reached the safety of the narrow ravine when the Ambler managed to extract itself from the pile of rubble Vickers had rained down on it.

It began to fire on them immediately, and Lisa ordered the others to randomize their movements as much as they could—right before she took a bullet herself.

It hit her in the upper back, and the shock and impact of it sent her to her knees as she muffled a scream with the back of her hand.

Ahead, the mouth of the ravine swam in the heat, as though taunting her.

So close...so far.

Rug swung her head to register what had happened, and when she did, the Quatro's eyes went wide. "*Lisa Sato!*" she hissed.

With that, she about-turned, faster than Lisa would have thought possible for a Quatro. Then she ran back toward the Ambler, rearing up to place her paws on a steep rise.

"Help her, Rodney Vickers!" Rug yelled without turning. "I will hold off this metal beast for as long as I can."

"Rug," Lisa managed to yell. "No!"

"Go, Lisa Sato. I will not behave recklessly in this. But I also refuse to let this contraption cut our friendship short."

Nothing can cut our friendship short, Rug. No matter what happens.

But Lisa accepted Vickers' help at last, and she hobbled stiffly over the uneven terrain.

Thankfully, the land trended mostly downward. Even so, Vickers had to help her descend by holding the back of her jumpsuit for as long as he could before she touched down.

It wasn't long before they had to go down over a rise large enough that she had to drop for more than a meter.

When she hit the ground, spasms of pain racked her body, and she was unable to keep her footing. She shook on the ground, hands curling uselessly at nothing.

Vickers landed beside her, and he didn't ask whether she was ready to continue—he simply hoisted her up by her armpits and they kept hobbling along, somehow.

She was glad he didn't ask. It was exactly how she wanted the soldiers she'd trained to act, actually. Wasting time on mercy or sympathy at a time like this would only kill Rug, or possibly all three of them. Either Lisa could make it in time or she couldn't, and it would be much better if she could.

At last, they reached the ravine, and Lisa immediately opened up a wide channel, not bothering to take the time to configure a two-way: "Rug! We're in! Now you come back, too."

But the Quatro was already bounding toward them across the terrain, armor-piercing rounds from the Ambler's twin autocannons tearing up the ground all around her.

Lisa had Vickers help her scrabble away from the entrance to the ravine—just in time. Rug barreled through, arresting her momentum several meters in.

"Let's keep going," Lisa said. "We're still not completely safe."

As though to confirm her words, more bullets bit into the rock face of the ravine mouth, sending flecks of stone flying through the air.

It took them an hour more at Lisa's hobbled pace to get back to the shuttles, where the rest of the militia awaited them, unharmed.

Lisa's chest swelled with pride, then—at her own actions.

It's okay to take pride in your own work, her father's voice told her inside her head. In her own voice, she added: *Especially when that work results in saving your friends.*

"We need to send a shuttle for Tessa," Lisa said through gritted teeth. "I'll go with that shuttle. Rug, you can stay with the one we came in, and we'll return with its pilot soon."

The Quatro studied her with solemn eyes. "No, Lisa Sato. I would share a shuttle with you and Tessa Notaras once more."

Returning the alien's gaze, Lisa marveled at the magnanimity of the Quatro—the capacity to forgive.

If we were all like Rug, the world would be a much happier, much safer place.

"All right, then. Come on."

Lisa ordered their new shuttle pilot to take the long way around to pick up Tessa and the rogue pilot. She didn't feel like having to worry about Ambler fire twice in one day.

They found Tessa and the pilot exactly where Tessa had said they'd be, and as usual, the older woman had the situation well in hand. The pilot sat with his hands over the back of his head, which was tucked between his knees.

"Look at me," Lisa ordered, her voice cold. She leaned against Rug, who'd tried to tell her to stay inside the shuttle, but she'd insisted on coming out.

The pilot refused to budge.

"Look at her, Slime," Tessa said, and now the pilot did look. The white-haired soldier smiled. "I've been passing the time by teaching him to heed me."

"He'd better learn to heed all of us," Lisa said, her voice strained.

Tessa squinted at her. "You all right?"

"I'm *fine.*"

"She's been shot, Tessa Notaras," Rug said.

"I see. We'd better get that seen to, then." Tessa paused, studying the Quatro with wary eyes. "How are *we*, Rug?"

"We remain part of the same drift, and our friendship remains intact."

Bowing her head, Tessa said, "Thank you. Thank you, so much."

"You've got some guts," Lisa said to the pilot, her voice even tighter. "You knew about that Ambler being down there, didn't you?"

The pilot didn't answer, his face looking paler by the second.

"He did," Tessa said. "He told me all about it while we waited. Came to find himself very loose-tongued during our time together, did Slime."

Lisa decided not to probe too deeply into that statement. "We still need him to fly the shuttle," she said. "But we need to start double-checking everything he claims."

"Oh, I doubt he'll try something like that again," Tessa said. She paused before adding, somewhat grudgingly: "But I see the wisdom in what you're saying."

Inside the shuttle, Tessa inspected Lisa's bullet wound. "Your shoulder's a mess. Looks like the round only clipped it, though—it didn't actually go through. Otherwise, you wouldn't have a shoulder anymore. Those autocannons fire armor-piercers."

"Can you do anything for it?"

"I can dress it, in the old-fashioned way. Iatric nanobots would be ideal, but since we don't have a nanotechnician with us, we'll have to make do with what we can scrounge from the medkits."

Within a half hour, they were underway again—hundreds of feet in the air, scanning the terrain for signs of the Gatherer convoy.

They picked it up again two miles past the ravine where they'd encountered the Ambler. This time, Lisa and Tessa pored over the landscape themselves, looking for signs of enemies.

They found none, so they decided to risk touching down and continuing their investigation. It was possible the same Ambler would find them again, but hopefully not. If it did, maybe they'd be able to finish it off, this time.

Lisa didn't actually believe that. But their mission was too important to suffer further delays.

"I think you should stay behind," Tessa said.

"Like hell," Lisa said. "I'm coming, too."

"*Lisa,*" Tessa said, leveling a characteristically stern glare at her.

"Don't try that with me, Tessa. I'm not a little girl anymore. I don't cling to your apron strings like I used to. Like it or not, I lead this militia, and I'm not being taken off this mission."

Tessa didn't argue any further, though Lisa did hear her mutter, "I'd look ridiculous in an apron."

The shuttles touched down, and they picked up the Gatherer trail once more.

After twenty minutes of trailing them, the Gatherers disappeared into a tunnel that was naturally concealed by the terrain—cast in shadow by an overhang.

"We're going in," Lisa said, and that was that.

Rug insisted on taking point, and Nail joined her, along with Pen, Fan, and most of the other Quatro that hadn't stayed behind to guard the shuttle pilots, all ten of whom they'd corralled inside the same shuttle for easy monitoring. Next came the human portion of the militia. The rest of the Quatro brought up the rear.

For a time, all that could be heard was the tromp of boots, the soft but audible padding of Quatro paws, and the skittering of the Gatherers.

Then, a scream broke the silence, from directly behind Lisa.

She whirled around, and she gasped, the shock causing fresh pain to shoot down her back, emanating from her injury.

One of the Gatherers had impaled Rodney Vickers.

CHAPTER 22

Shower of Shrapnel

Lisa reacted without thinking, switching her SL-17 to fully automatic and opening fire on the Gatherer attacking Vickers. She unloaded a full magazine into the thing, swapped in another one from her belt, and kept firing.

The Gatherer withdrew the thin blade with which it had skewered Vickers, turned to Lisa, and advanced toward her. Behind it, Vickers slumped to the tunnel floor, clutching his midsection and trailing blood down the rock wall.

Taking a step backward, Lisa continued to unload on the alien robot. At last, when she'd spent almost two full magazines on it, it burst apart in a shower of shrapnel, some of which *pinged* off the front of Lisa's jumpsuit.

She nearly tripped over the Gatherer behind her, then, and she dodged ahead just in time to evade the swipe of a claw, freshly grown just for her.

Accidents involving the Gatherers were not unheard of, and she'd read plenty of news reports about people losing property to the things. There'd even been a few people who'd lost their lives to the machines.

But other than clearing the path between whatever resources they were collecting and the deposit sites, the Gatherers had never been known to use their transforming ability to shape weapons for intentional use against foes of any kind.

Before this, Lisa had only known the robots to have one function.

Now, she knew better.

She managed to roll a sizable rock off the tunnel floor and into her hand, which she hurled at the Gatherer that was inching toward her, now wielding four claws, each at the end of a ropey, metallic limb.

The rock connected squarely with the thing, knocking it back, and causing the sinewy limbs to flail in a way that would have been comical under other circumstances.

Lisa reached for one of the grenades clipped to her belt, but thought better of it. In these tight confines, that would have endangered her companions. Instead, she resumed the same approach as before, peppering the thing with bullets while walking backward.

She still had to swap in a second magazine to finish the job, and the Gatherer surged forward as she did. When her back connected with the rock face, panic surged through Lisa, and she desperately tried to click the magazine into place.

At last, she got it, opening fire. This Gatherer only took two rounds from the second clip before exploding.

Either the rock helped, or my aim's getting better.

She spotted Rug to her right, contending with three of the beasts. The Quatro blasted one clean apart with her energy weapon, and then she swiped at another as it leapt toward her, knocking it into the rock and causing it to shatter in a satisfying cascade of sparks and shrapnel.

Even though Rug had vanquished it, the second Gatherer had managed to bloody Rug's paw, and the third latched onto her side, ripping savagely into flesh.

Wincing, Lisa fired at the thing, praying she didn't harm her friend in the process.

She got one round in before Rug yelled, "*Stop!*"

Lisa did, and the Quatro slammed the Gatherer against the rock—once, twice.

The robot finally disintegrated with the second blow.

"Let me see," Lisa said, reaching for Rug's side, which glistened with blood in the dim light provided by their jumpsuits.

"No time," Rug said, charging at a Gatherer that was menacing Tessa. The Quatro batted it against the wall, where it exploded.

Nodding at Rug, Tessa turned to fire on another Gatherer with a shotgun.

Ten minutes later, the battle was over, with all the Gatherers destroyed.

But not without exacting an awful toll on Lisa's militia. When she finally made it to him, Rodney Vickers stared into space with glassy eyes. Lisa was just closing his eyelids with her fingers when she heard a shriek from behind her.

She turned to see Beatie Anderson—a good soldier—holding her own intestines in her hands.

"End it," Anderson moaned. "Please, please."

Lisa shot a glance behind her shoulder, feeling helpless.

I can't do this. No way I can do this.

Her gaze found Tessa, who was already walking past, her features tightening as she drew her pistol to place it against Anderson's head.

"Goodbye, friend," Tessa said. "You served well."

Anderson only sobbed, until the shot rang out, and she fell backward, her skull glancing off a rock with a sickening *crack.* She still clutched her innards between her fingers.

Turning to face Lisa, Tessa reholstered her pistol.

"I—" Lisa said, and it came out as a croak. Her chin wobbled, and she felt like sitting on the tunnel floor and crying.

You lead these people, Lisa Sato. Get it together. Now.

"This..." She swallowed. "What does this mean? The Gatherers...they've never..."

"It means things just got a lot more dire on this planet," Tessa answered, and Lisa thought she could hear the "girl" that she didn't add. "And we've only just arrived."

Rug joined them. "We must move forward. If these Gatherers were reprogrammed by my people to bring more resources to them, then those Quatro could be in danger. More will be coming."

Lisa nodded, wiping her eyes on her upper arm. "Neutralize every Gatherer we encounter. We won't let them travel among us like that anymore. They won't get that advantage again."

She didn't know whether the others found her words comforting, but they did nothing for her, personally. They couldn't bring back Vickers, or Anderson.

Checking over her assault rifle, she moved to take the lead as they progressed down into the pitch-black of underground.

CHAPTER 23

Cordage

As fast as the **MIMAS** mechs were, the quads were faster, and so, it seemed, were the Quatro in general.

We've never had the problem of having to chase them before, Ash reflected.

Probably, Chief Roach would have been able to catch up to them on his own, but he seemed newly attuned to the need for Oneiri Team to continue functioning as a united force.

Facing down fifty plus Quatro will do that.

That said, Roach had performed more than admirably while taking on three quads simultaneously. Even before fusing with the alien mech, the man had possessed battle calm in spades, but now his movements spoke of an entity that *interfaced* with battle, making it dance to a tune he played.

The moment they'd lost sight of their quarry, Marco had projected the enemy's probable trajectory and deduced that they were headed straight for Cordage, another Glades village.

"I wonder if it's a fluke, that their escape route is taking them toward another settlement," Henrietta said when Marco shared the news.

"I doubt it, Razor," Roach said. "I'd bet the Quatro have extensive intel on this area."

Again, Roach surprised Ash by using the nickname she'd only just come up with for Henrietta Jin.

He really is making an effort to reintegrate with the team.

She experienced a glimmer of hope, then.

Maybe we can win this thing, after all.

They reached the village as dawn was breaking, the trees thinning once more, giving way to structures. Now that she could see them without engaging her night vision, and she had time to actually study them for a second, Ash saw that the homes were designed to match the forest, with logs that had not been cut to give that right-angle, rectangular look most buildings had. Instead, they cascaded down the buildings in waves. Somehow, the resulting aesthetic managed to appear elegant rather than ramshackle.

There was no sign of Quatro anywhere, though Ash now knew better than to take that as a reason to relax.

Still, a few villagers had already emerged from their homes into the early morning. The first person Oneiri came across was cutting wood behind what was presumably her home.

When she noticed the mechs approaching, she dropped her ax, wavering as though about to flee, her skin paling.

"You," Roach barked. "Have there been any sign of Quatro around here?" He said it as though she wasn't looking at them like they were a host of demons descending on her village for the sole purpose of wreaking havoc and bringing torment.

Her voice shook as she answered: "N-no, sir. No Quatro here."

Roach grunted, marching past her, causing the pile of wood she'd stacked to tremble with each step. With the third step, it toppled over.

Crouching near the woman, Ash restacked the wood, though she wasn't sure the new pile resembled the old one very much. The logs felt likes twigs beneath her metal fingers, and she was having trouble with the delicate motions the operation required.

She stood up again, clearing her throat. "Uh—don't mind Dynamo, ma'am. Diplomacy never was his strong suit. I'm Steam." She was about to extend her hand before thinking better of it, fearful that she'd crush the woman's tiny digits in her grasp.

"Bethany," the woman said, mouth agape.

Ash exchanged looks with Beth, who stood nearby. Beth's MIMAS tilted its head sideways.

"Bethany," Ash said, smiling inside her mech. "What a nice name."

They followed Roach through to the center of the village, where he was in the midst of questioning another villager.

The man quaked where he stood, and the rest of the village green was conspicuously empty of other villagers.

I wonder why, Ash thought sarcastically as she heard a door slam shut nearby.

Inserting herself between the alien mech and the man as carefully as she could, Ash craned her neck to stare up at the behemoth Roach had become.

"Uh, sir? Hi. What have you discovered?"

"I was just in the middle of asking this guy about the Quatro." Roach moved his hand, as though to nudge Ash out of the way.

"Uh, yes," she said, catching his hand by the wrist. "But—it doesn't look like the Quatro have been here, does it? I'm not sure further questioning is necessary."

"Hmm," Roach said. "I guess not. We should search the surrounding terrain."

"Good! Good idea. Let's let these people get back to their daily tasks."

Nodding curtly, Roach turned to march off the village green.

The man's gaze switched rapidly back and forth from Roach to Ash to Roach again. Behind him, a Gatherer trundled toward a collection facility.

"Have a nice day, sir," she said. "Best wishes." She snapped off a jaunty little salute and followed the chief.

God. That was awful. Looks like I'm getting pretty terrible at diplomacy myself.

A scream rose up behind her, and she turned, extending her bayonets instinctively.

The Gatherer had abandoned its course toward the collection facility to tackle the man. It reared above him, blades snaking out from its ever-shifting surface.

Ash didn't think—she just acted. Her right hand segmented, retracting to rest against her wrist, and she spun up that rotary autocannon. Armor-piercing rounds caught the Gatherer in the side, causing it to disintegrate instantly.

Shaking even worse than before, the man managed to regain his feet.

"Are you hurt, sir?" Ash called.

"N-no..." he said, staring down at himself. "I don't think..."

She turned back to Roach, who'd stopped just beyond the village green, standing perfectly immobile in that somewhat creepy way he had.

Neither of them said anything.

Slowly, Ash turned to see how the other MIMAS pilots were reacting.

They were also standing stock-still, and though Ash couldn't see their expressions, she'd become accustomed enough to their body language while inside the mechs that she could tell they felt as shocked as she did.

Marco was the first to speak:

"The ramifications of this...they really, really don't look good."

You said a mouthful.

CHAPTER 24

Crescedo

Something strange happened when Jake beheld the ruins of his childhood home.

As he was beginning to become accustomed to, the alien mech dream represented his anguish in a number of novel ways. In addition to the rising minor note played by a long-neglected violin, it also treated him to the sensation of bugs crawling all over his skin, coating him completely. Writhing there, as though they were a second suit that separated his physical body from the mech.

That caused his anguish to spike even more, which in turn caused the piercing violin note to crescendo more sharply, and it granted the insects tiny pincers, which they used to dig up small scoops of his skin, in a journey toward his organs that would be as slow as it was painful.

To top it all off, the dream granted him the sensation of breathing great lungfuls of tear gas.

The feedback loop continued for some time, resisting his every effort to arrest its escalation.

Finally, he lost control entirely. He charged across the gently curving terrain in great leaps and bounds, straight toward his wrecked childhood home.

His mounting rage and torment obliterated all thought, all consciousness, even though he remained aware of everything he was doing.

The main difference was that he was no longer the one piloting the mech. Nor was the mech piloting itself—instead, his raging emotions alone steered his actions. In part, he was fleeing those emotions, and in larger part, he was channeling them.

The Ravagers began to notice his charge, and as they did they scampered across the fields toward him. They, too, appeared to enjoy gravity inside the comet.

Some of the robots directly overhead used their powerful legs to try leaping past the artificial sun, in an attempt to skip the terrain they'd otherwise have to cross to reach Jake. The first few that tried it were jerked downward again by gravity.

Then, one of them made it—it jumped high enough to reach the tip of the spire that held the artificial sun aloft, so that gravity reversed its pull, sending the Ravager hurtling toward Jake.

His right arm became a massive pillar, which he swung in a broad arc, connecting with the robot as it fell and pulverizing it into fine dust.

The insects had acquired stingers in addition to their pincers, and they put them to use immediately, driving them into Jake's flesh at random intervals. The stingers seemed to produce a small quantity of venom—at least, if the subcutaneous fire Jake experienced was any indication.

Casting his gaze wildly around him, Jake saw that dozens more Ravagers raced across the comet toward him, along with several more who leapt against the gravity, attempting the same trick his first attacker had managed.

Within seconds, dozens of Ravagers became hundreds.

Where are they all coming from?

Had they been hiding inside the dying woods? Were they burrowed inside the thirty meters of soil that separated the comet's living space and its icy exterior, providing nutrients for crops and protecting against space radiation?

It was a mystery he lacked the time to solve. The first wave of Ravagers hit him, and he became a windmill of death, four blades protruding from him to slice through robot after robot as he spun around and around. Some of them disintegrated as the first one had, and others merely exploded to send machine parts hurtling across the land, each arm or leg or elbow or servomotor flying like a baseball hit by a home-run slugger.

More Ravagers hit him from above, then, and Jake retracted the blades so that he could bring his hands into play once again, though enlarged slightly, making it all the easier to crush the robots the moment he caught them.

If he only crushed them a little, he could flick them at other oncoming robots, channeling all of his rancor into the throw and causing both robots involved to rupture in a fantastic blizzard of metal fragments.

Eventually, he killed enough Ravagers that they came to respect him, despite their kamikaze tendencies. They waited for their fellows to arrive, now, bunching together, no doubt in the hopes of overwhelming Jake in a single unified flood.

He would not have it. Instead, he ordered his arms to become cannons that were disproportionate with his body. In truth, they were ridiculously large, but it was also what his disproportionate emotions called for just then.

He began to blast the Ravagers, each shot representing incredible overkill. Every thick bolt of energy took out not only the target but several around it, leaving wide craters in the ground.

The thought occurred to Jake that he risked blowing holes in the comet itself, creating more openings to the void beyond. If he did that, he would make it harder for any survivors to turn the comet back into something that resembled their home.

There are no survivors, something whispered into his ear, and this time he was certain it wasn't his own thought, even though he acknowledged the truth of what it said. *There's only you and the death you deal. You'll die too, soon enough, but your death will be worthy.*

Jake didn't die—not then, anyway. He couldn't have said how long it took, but he managed to clear all of the Ravagers, and when the task was done he collapsed to the ground, the alien mech curling into a tight ball, clutching itself as the insects and the heat and the minor note overcame everything.

After an eternity, the pain subsided, and the insects receded into whatever dimension they'd come from.

Wearily, Jake dragged himself to his feet to trudge across the comet, across fields and through withering woods, until he arrived at the hidden emergency shelter that he knew was located near the Council chambers.

He used his implant to submit his identity as a native of this comet to the computer. It recognized him, and the wide, horizontal entrance slid open to admit him into the airlock, the grassy field that covered it splitting in two.

Gently, he lowered his mech into the chamber below. He had to crouch to allow the hatch to close again, and when it did, the chamber pressurized, filling with oxygen.

"Let me out," he ordered the mech.

Nothing happened.

"*Let me out!*"

It heeded him, this time, though he wasn't sure what had been different about his second request. A ramp lowered from the front of the mech, just as it had before, and Jake crawled out.

He used his implant to order the inner airlock door to lower—this one was vertical, and it led into the emergency shelter that served as the last resort for residents.

When the hatch sank low enough, it revealed the face of Brianne Price, her lower lip trembling.

"Jake," she mouthed, though he couldn't hear her voice over the *clank* of the hatch.

At last, it was open, and he ran to her.

CHAPTER 25

Definitely Fearless

Instead of searching the terrain surrounding the village, Roach decided they would remain to defend it instead.

Well, actually, Ash and the others had lobbied him to stay here, and at last he relented.

"It's possible the Gatherer attack was a freak malfunction," Ash had said. "And it may never happen again. But unlike the Amblers, they've never done anything like this before."

Inside his mech, Marco had nodded. "Plus, this was where we thought the Quatro were going to attack, and they still might. There haven't been any reports of them striking anywhere else. So let them come here."

"We're ready for them, all right," Henrietta said, raising her metal fists a little before dropping them by her sides once more.

"Maybe we should contact Bronson," Ash said. "About the Gatherers."

"Go ahead," Roach said. "I'm done with that asshole." With that, he walked away, headed for the perimeter of the village.

"Uh..." Henrietta said, watching him go. "I assume he's not going to leave on us?"

"I don't think so," Ash said, also staring at the alien mech's back. "I think he's back with Oneiri for good."

"Our fearless leader once more," Henrietta added.

"He's definitely fearless," Richaud said, before sauntering away himself, in the opposite direction.

Ash also left, strolling aimlessly throughout the village as she attempted to raise Bronson using her implant.

Before long, the captain walked alongside her in the dream, looking minuscule beside her mech, though carrying himself no less confidently for that.

"What can I do for you, Seaman Apprentice Sweeney?"

She glanced down at him. "Isn't it about time I got promoted to Seaman, sir?"

Staring up at her, the corner of Bronson's mouth quirked. "Processing promotions have gotten pushed to the back burner for now, I'm afraid. We've been unusually busy, lately."

"Fair enough," she said, nodding, although the fact that she'd commanded Oneiri Team in Roach's place seemed a little incongruous with her low rank. "I'm contacting you to report a strange incident with one of the Gatherers, here in Cordage. In short, it appeared to divert itself from the collection facility in order to randomly attack a resident."

"I see. Cordage doesn't have a Darkstream contract. Did you know that?"

"I...I'm afraid I don't see how that's relevant, sir."

"Well, I just think it would be useful for you to mention to them that if they had one, they wouldn't have to worry about attacks, from Gatherers or from anyone else. They could rest easy, even after Oneiri Team leaves."

Ash paused. "Is that an order, sir?"

"Sure. It's an order."

"All right, then." She resisted the urge to clear her throat, concerned it would serve as a vehicle for her true feelings about Bronson's words. "How is Jake, sir?"

"Price went rogue. I left him behind in the Belt."

She stopped walking. "You left him *behind?* How will he survive out there? Did you leave him with a shuttle and supplies? Does Darkstream have a jail out there, or something? What do you mean by 'left behind,' exactly?"

Peering up at her, Bronson said, "What do you mean, *sir.*"

"Yes, sir."

"I'm afraid the details of Price's defection are classified."

The dream pulsed to reflect Ash's accelerating heartbeat. "Sir...Jake Price is my teammate and my friend. I'd like to—"

"He's also the least of your concerns, Sweeney. You're in the middle of a war. Time to get it together."

To that, she had no reply.

"A report just came in that Peppertree is under attack by Quatro. That's near you, meaning it's almost certainly the group you recently encountered. Peppertree *also* doesn't have a contract with Darkstream. In fact, they switched to one with Red Company—an arrangement that's in the process of failing them. Your orders are to swoop in, save the day, and persuade the council there that renewing their contract with us is in their best interests. It's a double win: we reclaim our contract *and* we send a message to other villages about who really has their backs."

Ash shook her head. "Sir...with everything that's going on, is customer acquisition really our main concern, here?"

"Our *main concern,* Sweeney, is a strong Darkstream, and this helps us reinforce that. A strong Darkstream means a stable system and a safe people. Have you forgotten that?"

"No, sir," Ash muttered.

"Good. Now get going."

CHAPTER 26

Peppertree

Gabe had run out of time for Darkstream executives and officers, especially Captain Bob Bronson.

Nevertheless, their interests coincided with his for now, and there was no use denying that. For differing reasons, they both wanted Quatro dead, and Gabe was happy to make that happen.

So he didn't argue when Sweeney came to him with the proposed mission.

"Let's go," he said simply. "I want to leave now."

"Now" ended up meaning twenty minutes later, after Sweeney had gathered the rest of Oneiri from whatever parts of the village they'd wandered off to. They had to check over their mechs' critical systems, as well.

Gabe regarded them as they did so, remaining perfectly still, even though he felt excruciatingly restless.

He did end up developing a reservation about the mission, though, and it came in the form of Jess, appearing to him for the first time since he'd fused with the alien mech.

"Don't go to that village," Jess said, peering up at him, her face solemn.

He didn't react—he'd mastered his emotions better than that a long time ago, and he only ever reacted to stimulus he knew posed an immediate danger. No, he stayed just as steady and still as he had before.

Unfortunately, his stillness did not reflect an inner calm. What was left of his human body—its circulatory system and its nervous system—pulsed with tension, and a chorus of whispers rose up, uttering a multitude of contradictory statements, trying to jerk him every which way and yet in no direction at all.

"Well?" Jess asked. "Are you going to answer me? It's impolite to ignore someone after they've given you a warning."

It occurred to Gabe, suddenly, that this mech he'd joined with might have been made by allies of the Quatro. What if it was designed to corrupt him—to lead him astray with hallucinations like this one, which resembled his lost love exactly?

"You're not there," he ground out at last. "And you're not Jess. You're something that's trying to stop me from getting my revenge."

With that, Jess vanished, and Gabe looked beyond the spot where she'd been standing, to the rest of Oneiri.

They'd stopped whatever they'd been doing to stare at him. Sweeney's and Beth's heads were both cocked to the side.

"Sir...?" Henrietta Jin said. "You all right?"

"I'm fine," Gabe growled. "Are you ready or not?"

"Ready, sir," Richaud Lafontaine said, and the rest echoed the sentiment.

"Then let's go."

He took off into the woods, and his augmented hearing told him that behind him, the others followed, their footfalls displacing undergrowth and splintering roots.

At a full-on run, it took them fewer than thirty minutes to reach the village whose council had elected to switch their defense contract from Darkstream over to Red Company.

It wasn't hard to discern how that was working out for them. Quatro surrounded the small glade where the village had been built, firing on the structures where Red Company fighters were huddled, doing their best to return fire in the face of the brutal onslaught.

Oneiri Team got to work.

Gabe had no qualms about attacking the Quatro before they knew of his presence, and he knew the MIMAS pilots wouldn't, either. If a soldier didn't capitalize on every last advantage that presented itself, he wouldn't be doing his job.

His entire frame became a spinning blade of razor sharpness, cutting through three Quatro who'd arranged themselves conveniently in a row. His edge laid them open, causing scarlet viscera to plop out onto the ground, and Gabe assumed a humanoid shape once again as he completed the attack.

Too easy. Where are those quads?

He cast about for them, wading through the ranks of Quatro, dispatching the unclad Quatro almost as an afterthought.

If the Quatro had fled once again the moment they'd detected Oneiri's presence, that wouldn't have surprised him. But they didn't, and that *did* surprise him.

Instead of retreating, they redoubled their efforts, tightening the noose around Peppertree, charging between the buildings to savage the Red Company fighters with massive fangs and claws.

That only fed into Oneiri's efforts, and they tightened a noose of their own, closing in on the Quatro ranks to continue eviscerating them.

Still no quads to be found. Were they on the opposite side of the village? Why would they let their naked brethren fall in droves like this?

He turned to give Lafontaine the order to loop around the village in an attempt to track down the quads.

As he did, something *shifted.*

Richaud Lafontaine became a Quatro, slavering with its bloodlust.

Gabe was back in Northshire.

This time, he hadn't arrived too late—after the Quatro had finished with their slaughter.

No, this time, he was here *as they were carrying it out.*

Another key difference: Gabe wasn't in his old body, as he had been at that time. For this do-over, he instead had access to the sheer might of the alien mech.

Gabe's arms became massive energy cannons, and he aimed them at the Quatro that Lafontaine had become.

No. Stop this. This isn't real.

But it really did seem he was back on Northshire's village green, just in front of the mayor's residence. Jess Sweeney walked out of the front door, resplendent in her white summer dress.

As Gabe tried to call to her, his voice catching in his throat, Jess descended the stairs from the porch and began to cross the village green.

"Jess, no!" Gabe managed to cry, just as her eyes fell on the massive Quatro that awaited her.

The beast charged, and Gabe opened fire with his energy cannons. Massive beams of impacted with the Quatro's flank, creating charred, gaping holes.

The Quatro hit the dirt, unmoving, but another Quatro was running at Jess—this one with bright blue eyes. Gabe shifted his autocannons toward it.

Wait. Quatro don't have blue eyes.

Everything flashed, the Northshire village green vanishing for a moment to reveal the battle around Peppertree.

The Quatro he'd trained his autocannons on became Ash Sweeney—but only briefly.

Northshire replaced the scene once more, and Sweeney became the Quatro that was advancing on Jess.

Do I fire?

The world flashed again, becoming Peppertree. Then it reverted to Northshire, and the process repeated several times more.

For a period of several long seconds, Peppertree reappeared, and Gabe saw Lafontaine's mech lying on the ground, blackened and smoking.

The mech dream pulsed with Gabe's horror as he checked Lafontaine's vitals.

He was dead.

With that, Gabe turned away from Peppertree and fled into the woods.

CHAPTER 27

Lockdown Mode

After they got the typical mother-seeing-her-son-for-the-first-time-in-years stuff out of the way—complete with comments on how much he'd changed, and facial expressions that mixed wonderment and anxiety in equal measure—Jake wanted to see his sister. Before he saw to anything else, he wanted that.

"Of course," his mother said, tears still clinging to her eyes. "Come with me."

He followed her through a sterile, metal corridor, from which you could access everything inside the emergency shelter. At least, if his memories of the frequent drills of his youth were any indication.

Along the way, he received greetings from neighbors he barely remembered, as well as from a man and a woman he recognized as Council members. They'd barely spared a moment's thought for him, back when he'd been growing up here, but now their breathless words were delivered in tones of reverence.

Jake didn't care. He only wanted to see Sue Anne.

Space inside the emergency shelter was fairly limited, but because of her condition, Sue Anne had gotten her own room.

Brianne entered first, leaving the door slightly ajar while Jake waited in the hallway.

"Sue...you have a visitor. Sue?"

Muffled whispering from the sickroom, accompanied by the soft beeping of a heart monitor.

Footsteps recrossed the room, nearing the door, and Brianne appeared once more, wearing a smile that looked in danger of getting blown away by the slightest breeze.

"Okay. I'll leave you two to catch up."

"Thanks, Mom." He hugged her again, for the eleventh time since he'd arrived, and then he went in to see his sister.

He stopped just two feet into the room.

It had been months since Sue Anne had been well enough to record video messages to accompany the ones his mother frequently sent him. During that time, she'd ceased to be his sister and had become a pasty, thin creature without any hair.

The creature's mouth broadened in a smile that looked truly pleased, but the eyes...the eyes were so, so tired.

"S-Sue Anne?" he croaked, and knew right away that the uncertainty in his voice was exactly the wrong reaction.

"Yes," she said, her voice a barely audible rasp. "Of course it's me. Come closer."

He did, and each step felt heavy, as though he were marching toward his own funeral.

"How...?" Jake cleared his throat. "How do you feel?"

It was perhaps the dumbest question he could have asked. Possibly, it was the dumbest question *anyone* had ever asked.

Obviously she feels awful.

"Today isn't the worst day," she said, maintaining her smile.

"That's good," he said, trying for a natural-looking smile himself, but he knew he was feeling miserably. It felt like a pasted-on grin.

Worse, he couldn't think of a single thing to talk about. What could he possibly ask his sister that would be relevant, or even kind?

Every question that popped into his head struck him as callous, frivolous.

What have you been up to?

What do you do for kicks?

See any good movies lately?

Have you been following the war on Eresos? A lot of people are dying, hey?

"It's okay, Jake," she said, and her smile had taken on a note of true sympathy—as if *he* were the one deserving of pity in this situation.

Incredible!

"You don't have to say anything. Just sit, why don't you? It's good to see you."

But instead, he took a step backward, toward the door. He cleared his throat again.

"I should really—um, the Council will want to see me. They'll need the airlock fixed, so that it goes into Lockdown Mode, and they can start reclaiming the surface..."

"Of course," Sue Anne said, nodding. "Go do that. That needs to take priority—people getting back to normal life. We'll talk when you've taken care of it. Love you, Jake."

"Love you, Sue Anne." And with that, he fled the sickroom.

His stomach roiled, and heat prickled all along his spine. The back of his throat burned, too.

What was *that?*

His mother was waiting with Councilman Ryan Pichenko.

"Jake!" Pichenko said, extending his hand. "What's it like to be home?"

He stared at the hand for a moment, then shook it.

"Are you all right, Jake?" his mother asked.

"Yes," he said, trying to force his mind back to normal functioning, recoiling from his own guilt over the way he'd behaved toward his sister. "I'm fine. How...how did you survive the attack?"

Pichenko answered. "Comet Seven was attacked first, on the opposite side of Hub. Ours was hit not long after, but we got lucky—at least, luckier than some of the other comets. We had just enough warning to get almost half of the residents inside the shelter."

"Only half?" Jake asked in disbelief.

Pichenko lowered his head, with what appeared to be authentic sadness tugging at the corners of his mouth. After working for Darkstream for so long, Jake found it odd to see actual emotion on the face of someone in a position of power.

"I'm afraid so, Jake. The other council members and I, we tried our best given the warning we had, but...it wasn't good enough."

Jake laid a hand on his shoulder. "You did what you could, Councilman. You're to be commended."

Pichenko met his eyes, and he actually seemed to appreciate the comment. "Thank you."

Why was that so easy, when talking to Sue Anne was so hard?

"It's possible other residents still survive, inside personal shelters," Jake said. "A few people had those, if I remember correctly, and they may have invited in neighbors."

Nodding, Pichenko said, "That's a good point. We should look into that immediately."

"First things first, though—I'll need to see what's gone wrong with the airlock's Lockdown Mode."

"Does that mean you'll have to get back inside that *thing?*" his mother asked, and when Jake looked at her, he got the sense that she'd blurted it out without thinking.

"Yes, Mom. I'm afraid it does."

CHAPTER 28

Defeatist

Lisa had taken the lead through the dark tunnels as a show of strength, but she didn't have the courage to back it up.

"You need to move faster," Tessa told her, thankfully subvocalizing so the others couldn't hear. "You're toeing through these caves like you're blind. If we don't speed up, another group of Gatherers will catch up to us."

It was certainly dark enough that Lisa *would* have been blind, had it not been for her implant's night vision capabilities. "Tessa," she subvocalized back, "I—I think I've lost my nerve." It was hard to confess that, and she wouldn't—couldn't—say it to the rest of the militia, for fear it would obliterate morale. "The Gatherers behaving so violently...it's totally unprecedented. Do you think we should start preparing for the possibility that we won't even make it back to oppose Darkstream?"

That brought a sharp look from the white-haired woman. "How in Sol do we prepare for *that?* Are you suggesting we prepare for our own deaths? That's defeatist, Lisa, and it's not how I trained you to behave. I trained you to act like a soldier."

Lisa glared back at the white-haired woman. "If the Gatherers are attacking us now, I don't see what hope there is for *anyone* on Eresos. And if the Amblers mount an organized assault—"

"You're letting your imagination run wild."

"Are you saying it's not possible?"

"Of course it's possible. But if you spend your energy on obsessing over a scenario that has shown no sign of actually coming true, then you'll have none left over to deal with the scenario actually facing us."

Lips tightening, Lisa tried to ignore Tessa and refocus on the mission. Though the woman was grating on her, their conversation had had the benefit of making Lisa feel more angry than scared. She studied the route her implant had traced through the tunnels, so that they could find their way back.

The implant had also noted plenty of branching tunnels, but Lisa had continued to follow the Gatherers—or at least, the signs that they were still on a Gatherer path.

They didn't actually see any more Gatherers, which had been her intention. Catching up to the robots ahead would be just as bad as letting the ones behind catch up to them.

But the Gatherers always left little signs of their passage behind—mineral fragments they'd dropped along the way, scrapes along the rock that marked their paths, and so on.

We're on the right track. We have to be.

They were passing another branching tunnel when Tessa suddenly disappeared inside it, as though jerked sideways by some invisible force.

"Tessa?" Lisa yelled, panic filling her voice. She pointed her assault rifle into the side tunnel, which also angled the flashlight she'd mounted on her SL-17 in that direction.

The beam found Tessa suspended in the air before the dark silhouette of a four-legged beast.

A profound sense of déjà vu struck Lisa, then, from a time back on Alex, when they'd been manipulated by a similarly invisible force, using the metals in their pressure suits.

Quatro.

Something yanked her assault rifle out of her grasp, and the beam of light it projected rotated wildly, illuminating parts of the cave at random.

Lisa lost sight of Tessa.

Then, something slammed her against the rock from behind, and everything went black—even blacker than it had already been.

CHAPTER 29

Cascade Error

To investigate what had gone wrong with Comet Four's airlocks, Jake needed to travel to Hub's control center—the "hub" for which the city-settlement was named. It was made from a comet much smaller than the others.

After hours of trial and error, he was finally able to engage the Lockdown Mode for Comet Four's landing bay. He wasn't sure why the emergency safeguard hadn't kicked in, except that something had caused a cascade error in the system.

Luckily, the comet's computer systems were all isolated from each other, and so the error hadn't spread to other systems, such as Life Support, which kicked in with massive zirconia electrolyzers as soon as it detected that comet integrity had been achieved.

His job done, he departed Hub's control center, which thankfully had not been attacked. Its airlock functioned flawlessly, and so Jake had been able to access the computers while outside of his alien mech. Doing so with the giant mech's appendages would have proved tedious.

It would take the better part of a week for the electrolyzers to fill the entire comet with oxygen, but a lot of the residences had much smaller electrolyzers of their own, and by late afternoon on the day Jake engaged Lockdown Mode, a lot of residents were able to don pressure suits and leave the emergency shelter for their homes.

Out of thanks to Jake, Councilman Ryan Pichenko had lent his house to Brianne and Sue Anne Price indefinitely.

"I'll sleep in the Council Chambers," Pichenko said. "There are plenty of synthleather couches there that are more than comfortable enough for me to catch some shuteye."

"Thank you, Councilman," Jake said, giving Pichenko's hand a squeeze as they shook. "It means more than I can say."

"So does making the comet livable again. That means a lot to all of us. I'm far from repaying the debt we all owe you, Jake."

"No debt needs to be paid," Jake said. "This is my home, too." *At least, it was.* "I plan to check the other comets for survivors next."

Now, he sat with his mother in Pichenko's kitchen, with bowls of canned tomato soup sitting on the table in front of them. Outside the kitchen window, Jake's mech sat, inert, waiting for him to come and take command of it.

He didn't trust the thing. Not so long ago, he'd been locked in desperate combat with it, while it did its best to end his life. Now, it sat there like an obedient dog, waiting for its master to come and give it its next command.

Who would build a thing like that? And what's its purpose?

Did humanity have a guardian angel somewhere in the cosmos, designing unrivaled weapons for human use against their enemies?

Or did the alien mechs have another purpose?

"Where did you get that thing?" Brianne asked, following his gaze outside to the alien mech, a spoonful of soup halfway to her lips.

"It's an experimental Darkstream design," Jake lied.

It felt awful to deceive his mother, but Brianne had enough problems without worrying about alien invaders, or about the worrying effect Jake knew the alien mech was having on his psyche.

Unfortunately, Brianne wasn't buying it.

"There's no way humanity has technology that begins to approach that thing," she said. "Not even Darkstream. Besides, it looks exactly like photos of the one you and your father found on that comet. Don't lie to me, Jake. Is this mech the one you found?"

Jake shook his head slowly. "No," he said. "Someone else has that one."

"Where did you find this one, then?"

Jake hesitated, unsure whether he was supposed to divulge that information. At last, he said, "Dad didn't tell you he found a second mech?"

Instead of eating the soup in her spoon, Brianne lowered it back to the bowl, and her eyes found the tabletop. "Your father and I don't talk much, anymore, I'm afraid."

"Seriously?" This was news to Jake. "Why not?"

"I want him to come home, to be with Sue Anne, during her..." Brianne swallowed. "Peter thinks it's his duty to continue working, no matter what happens, to give Sue Anne the best possible chance, but it's..." Again, his mother couldn't finish.

It's only a matter of time, Jake finished for her, though he wouldn't dare to do so out loud.

CHAPTER 30

DuGalle

Before Roach turned on them, Oneiri had been wreaking havoc on the Quatro attacking Peppertree. Of the original fifty-six—a count that included the quads—a mere nineteen remained, by Ash's estimation, which she confirmed by instructing an AI to review the battle recordings from each MIMAS' point of view.

We were winning. And now this.

They buried Richaud Lafontaine at the edge of the glade that contained the village, beneath one of the taller trees, whose cascading branches formed a protective canopy over the grave.

Most of the villagers turned out for the funeral, probably out of gratitude for Oneiri saving their hides.

It really is the least they could do.

Ash was still too shell-shocked from Roach's bizarre betrayal and the loss of Richaud to say anything at the service they held.

Beth rose to the occasion once more, though, and the eulogy she gave ended up reminding Ash of the one at Tommy's funeral.

Mostly because we neglected to give Richaud a nickname before he died, too.

He'd been the last one not to receive one, and Ash had even been working some over in her mind, trying to decide between them.

At Tommy's funeral, they'd granted him a nickname posthumously, but they didn't do that at Richaud's. Ash suspected that Beth felt too ashamed on all of Oneiri's behalf, and Ash shared that sentiment.

It's too late. We lost him, and we clearly didn't appreciate him while he was here.

Marco and Henrietta had remained inside their mechs for the service, and Beth's and Ash's hadn't been far. Once Beth finished speaking, Henrietta stepped forward to plant the cross Beth had fashioned, driving it firmly into the ground with large, metal fists.

With that done, Ash and Beth got back inside their mechs, and Oneiri trudged back to the village.

"I'm going to kill Roach," Henrietta said as they passed the outer buildings. "If we see him, stay away from him. He's mine."

"The kill belongs to whoever manages to take him down, Razor," Ash said. The others already seemed to look at her as their leader, and she was doing her best to rise to the task, though her self-doubt ran deep. "We'll be lucky if we can manage it at all."

"Why did he do it?" Beth said. "How *could* he?" Her voice hitched as she asked the question none of them could answer. "Has he been with the enemy from the start?"

Marco shook his MIMAS' head. "We can't understand Roach's thinking any longer. He's more machine than man, now—much more. Maybe some hidden subroutine told him that killing Richaud was a logical step."

"A step toward *what?*" Henrietta said.

No one answered.

Darkstream had classified every Red Company fighter as enemy combatants, but in the confusion and distress following the engagement, no one from Oneiri had thought to make prisoners of the mercenaries that survived.

Doesn't seem like it's necessary, anyway.

The Red Company fighters appeared totally dejected, avoiding eye contact with everyone as they wandered aimlessly—especially with the villagers, who they'd convinced to let Red Company protect them, and who they'd utterly failed.

Now, Ash began to question the members of Red Company, to see who they had here, and also what they knew.

"You'll want to talk to DuGalle," said the bedraggled woman Ash asked first, who sat in the middle of what looked like someone's flower garden.

"Who's that?"

"The leader of Red Company, as near as we can tell. Our command structure has been almost totally wiped out, and everyone above DuGalle has been either confirmed or presumed dead. Saul was the last one to rank higher than him, but now that Saul's dead, DuGalle leads Red Company."

"Saul..." The name certainly rang a bell. Ash racked her brain, and finally she hit on it: he'd been the one in charge of the mercenaries at New Gower, back when Oneiri had first encountered Red Company. "He died? How?"

The woman raised her eyebrows. "As far as I know, you killed him. Outside Ingress. He was the one piloting the MIMAS we took off you."

So that's who that bastard was. Saul was the one who took Tommy's mech.

"Where's DuGalle, then?"

"Village green, last I knew."

"Thanks." Ash turned to stroll in that direction. Inside the MIMAS, even a stroll meant moving at a fair clip, and she took care to ensure she did no harm, either to property or to humans.

Without turning back, Ash said, "Saul deserved to die."

A brief pause. "Probably true," the woman called after her.

DuGalle was leaning against a fence, staring into space, looking just as lost as the rest of his comrades. A faded jean jacket hung over his thin frame, too large for him, and he had a thick French accent.

"How can I do for you, mech?" he asked, not bothering to look up at her.

The combination of expressions threw Ash off for a second. "Let me start by letting you know that Darkstream owns Peppertree's contract again. Are we going to have any problems over that?" Ash gestured with her right hand as she spoke, which was pretty significant coming from a MIMAS. It certainly drew DuGalle's gaze.

"No problems," he said. "Red Company is done, now, anyway. I don't see how we can recover."

"Done? You're giving up?"

"It's not a matter of giving up. Call it what it is: defeat. We overplayed our hand. Saul is dead, I'm in charge, and I can see that we're done. Quatro in their own mechs, the Quatro in general, rumors of Gatherers turning against the very villagers they made prosperous—if anyone can protect people from all that, it isn't us. Maybe Darkstream can."

"I see." Ash tilted her head back slightly, and the servomotors in her neck emitted a soft whine. "Well, I want you to know that I agree completely. You're totally ineffective, and I support you in acknowledging your uselessness."

She turned to leave, about to open a coms channel with Bronson to tell him the good news about Red Company.

"Darkstream overplayed its hand too, you know," DuGalle said. He hadn't bothered to raise his voice, but the MIMAS' enhanced hearing had automatically jacked up the volume for her benefit.

She stopped, glancing over her shoulder at him.

"You—how do you say—bit off more than you can chew. Much more."

Sighing, Ash turned and walked back to DuGalle, on the verge of plucking him from the fence he reclined against and shaking him till his teeth rattled out of his skull. "If you don't start saying something relevant within the next five seconds, you're going to seriously regret wasting my time."

"Certainly, mech. Darkstream deliberately started this war. Okay? Does this do anything for you?"

"The war started when Quatro attacked Northshire. That's the village I'm from, *mercenary*. They killed my family, and Darkstream has been working ever since to make sure they can never do something like that again."

DuGalle held up a finger. "First of all, you too are a mercenary, are you not?" A second finger went up. "Second, you are a very naive mech. Darkstream is not the noble victim in this conflict. As I said, they began this war themselves, on purpose. How do I know this, you should probably be asking? I'll tell you: Darkstream *paid* Red Company to put on company uniforms and attack the Quatro in their homes. After almost two decades of peace, give or take, Darkstream hired us to stir things back up again. To anger the aliens—by killing their families, and prompting them to seek revenge against all humans."

"Ridiculous," Ash said, though the dream had begun to pulse with her quickening heartbeat. "That doesn't even make any sense."

"Why, it makes perfect sense. Have Darkstream contracts not flourished? Have company profits not soared? They are back to their own tricks, is Darkstream—the tricks they first began to learn in the Milky Way. They've mastered them, by now. Would you like to know what Darkstream hired Red Company to do next?" DuGalle snickered. "Probably you would rather not know, because of how it will hurt your stupid head. But I'll tell you all the same. Once the Quatro were nice and pissed off, Darkstream paid us to go to the Quatro again—but not in company uniform, this time, and not to attack them. Instead, Darkstream gave us crates and crates of weapons. All kinds of weapons: medium machine guns, heavy guns, rocket and grenade launchers—all kinds! And what did Darkstream tell us to do with all that? They said, 'Give these to the Quatro and let's see what *they* do with them.'"

"I thought you said Red Company was over," Ash said, her tone indignant even as her voice wavered with uncertainty. "Yet here you are, trying to sway me with your propaganda."

Something pinged on Ash's HUD—a file transfer.

"Here is everything to back up what I'm saying. Copies of our orders from Darkstream, which the company demanded we destroy. Footage of conversations with company executives. And footage of the encounters with the Quatro; both the attack and the giving them the weapons. Why do I have all this neatly packaged together? Because Red Company's next step was to leak these documents, to delegitimize the company forever, in the eyes of everyone. But it is too late for us to do anything now. So here it is, for you to do with what you will."

As Ash stared at the transfer, afraid to open it, DuGalle pushed off of the fence and began to walk away.

"Where are you going?"

He turned, a sneer twisting his mouth. "I am leaving this place. Feel free to stop me—imprison or kill me. It doesn't matter. This planet goes to shit right now, mech, and my money rests on everyone who remains dying within the year."

CHAPTER 31

One-Note Dirge

The landing bay of the next comet over *had* engaged Lockdown Mode when the Ravagers had breached it, and Jake ordered the outer airlock open using the Hub-wide security clearance Pichenko had given him.

As he exited the airlock into the landing bay, his eyes fell on something that made him draw up short and stare, with the minor violin note rising again, keening shrilly until he wanted to claw at his ears.

Several residents of this comet, Comet Three, had attempted to reach a shuttle to escape. That shuttle had been blown apart, with a jagged hole yawning in its hull.

As for the people who attempted to flee...

Jake tried not to look at them as he walked by their ripped clothing and torn bodies, but he couldn't help it. He didn't recognize any of them as people he'd known growing up, but he wasn't sure he would've, even if they had been. Most of their faces had been pulped beyond recognition.

He progressed to the inner airlock, ordering it open to admit his mech.

This airlock was smaller than the outer one, which had been designed to admit small spacecraft. The inner airlock was meant mainly for people, as well as the occasional speeder or farm equipment that would have been brought through. As such, Jake would need to crawl through it, ignoring the voice that whispered for him to just blow a hole through it instead.

You're strong enough, the voice said. *Aren't you? Don't let them make you bow like this. Show them your might.*

Jake got to his knees and shimmied through the opening, trying to picture how ridiculous he must look: this huge, badass mech wiggling through a puny airlock.

It made him smile, and he needed that.

Even though this comet's integrity had remained intact, meaning it retained both atmospheric pressure and oxygen, its condition was far worse than Jake's home comet.

Here, every copse of trees had been put to the torch, and no structure had been left standing. Where the Council Chambers had once been, a crater stood in the ground.

From where Jake stood, the former site of the Chambers hung over his head, and the hole looked so deep that it seemed a miracle that whatever had created it hadn't blasted through the ice beyond.

Most of the homes hadn't received quite so thorough a treatment, though no matter where Jake looked—right, left, ahead, or up at the fields that served as his sky—he couldn't find a single one intact. The comet dwellings tended to take the shape of domes, but now they reminded him of cracked eggs.

He thought back to the shuttle inside the landing bay, and the damage that had been done to it.

Didn't seem like the work of the Ravagers, did it? he asked himself, and then he answered his own question: *No. Whatever did that was much bigger.*

And yet, he still hadn't spotted any enemies. Unlike his home comet, which had swarmed with Ravagers, this one was devoid of anything that moved.

He might have used his rockets to search the comet quickly, but he wanted to conserve the alien mech's fuel. He could replenish that with ease, but that would take more time, and time was an even more valuable resource than fuel, especially for any survivors still trying to hold out against the robot invasion.

So instead, Jake jogged across the terrain as it curved gently upward. Inside the alien mech, running still provided a fast way of getting around.

Before long, he happened upon a fenced-in field of livestock.

At least, that's what it used to be. The cows were all butchered, but not in a way that was useful to anyone.

Jake slowly shook his head. *Senseless.*

The ever-present voice had another thought, though: *Perhaps not—perhaps this slaughter did have a purpose. Perhaps this was the work of a weapon maintaining its edge.*

After ten minutes of fruitless searching through the countryside, Jake decided to head directly for the emergency shelter.

It opened for him without hesitation, the grassy halves parting with barely a whisper.

He'd just begun to lower himself down into the airlock when something surged up from below, knocking Jake backward to crash to the ground. The insects instantly returned, crawling all over Jake's body, a sea of skittering limbs and writhing carapaces and sharp pincers.

There's no one left alive in this comet...is there?

The violin resumed its one-note dirge.

He flipped over, regaining his feet to face his attacker—an alien mech that might as well have been a mirror image of the one he piloted.

The minor note turned into a minor chord, and the dream directed his attention upward, where something glinted in the artificial sun.

A second alien mech, hurtling through the comet under the power of its rockets, headed straight for him.

There was no time for Jake to form a plan. No time for him to think at all. The first mech charged.

CHAPTER 32

Charred Roots

When Lisa woke, the pain from her wounded shoulder had dimmed to a dull but steady throb.

She had to admit, Tessa had done a good job of dressing it, and it would probably heal up fine. In the meantime, Lisa refused to let it affect her performance.

Not that she had much cause to perform, right now.

Looking around using the dim light produced by her jumpsuit, she saw that the Quatro who'd captured them had converted one of their subterranean caves into a makeshift jail.

At least the cave's roomy. Lisa could give them that, but not much else.

There was nothing in the way of bedding, here. The floor was uneven, and attempting to sleep on it would be torture, if they were left here for that long.

The hours crawled by, and their Quatro captors treated them coldly. At first, they gave their prisoners nothing to eat. When a meal did come, it consisted of nothing more than a pile of charred roots, which Lisa ordered her militia to gnaw on nevertheless.

"We need to keep up our strength for when we escape," she told them, earning a grim smile from Tessa.

Their treatment seemed unnecessarily cruel, but then, when Lisa cast her mind back to when Rug's drift had captured and imprisoned them back on Alex, she supposed their treatment then had been similar to what they endured now.

Maybe this impersonality is simply what the language barrier leads to. That said, Rug had never knocked Lisa unconscious—she'd fainted upon capture on Alex, but the Quatro there had not been violent toward her. These Quatro had. Her aching head was evidence enough of that.

Either way, Rug and the other Quatro of Lisa's militia had not been imprisoned, and that gave Lisa hope that maybe an escape attempt would not be necessary.

That hope was soon dashed.

A Quatro Lisa didn't recognize soon appeared at the mouth of the cave, its body segmented by the crude metal bars that overlaid it.

Next to her captor stood Rug, though Lisa quickly noticed that she no longer wore the translator wrapped around her neck. Instead, the other Quatro wore it.

At that, a sweat broke out all over Lisa's skin. To lose the ability to speak to Rug, who had become such a dear friend after everything they'd endured together...it felt worse than if her jailor had struck her.

"Allow me to conjecture," the Quatro said, in a voice deeper than Rug's, which was already quite deep. "You're about to tell me that the Gatherers have attacked you and that we are all in very great danger."

Lisa cocked her head to the side. "Rug has already told you, then? Don't you trust her?"

"No. I am not quick to trust anyone, not even a fellow Quatro. This mistrusting is what has kept my drift alive for so long. Except to natural death, we have lost no members since being stranded on this wretched planet."

Lisa shook her head. "We came because we hoped to get your help. Your people are fighting and dying, far to the west of here."

"That may be true," the Quatro said, its orange eyes boring into Lisa's. "Or, it may be a two-leg trick, just as I suspect your tale about the Gatherers is."

Shooting a meaningful glance at Rug, Lisa said, "Rug has *four* legs. And she backs me up."

"She could easily be conspiring with you to trick us. I view everyone—Quatro or two-leg—who approaches us as potential Meddler agents, and you are certainly no different. This Quatro, who someone has apparently christened 'Rug,' is far from the first Quatro to come to us, seeking to 'unite the drifts.' She *is,* however, the first Quatro I've seen with access to the technology we all once wielded. I find it...*interesting* that the Meddlers did not take hers as it took ours.

"But I digress. We have heard about what the two-legs have done to the drifts that seek to unite with us, and we don't consider it in our best interests to unite with them, since we'd likely end up sharing in their suffering. And so we have prevented every single Quatro who came to us from ever returning to their original drifts, for fear that doing so would reveal our location. We will do the same with your friend, here, as well as the other Quatro who accompanied you. The entrance to these caves where we have made our home is also covered in bars. We have no wish to share in the suffering of other Quatro."

The line of argument that now seemed logical to Lisa was also one she'd vehemently argued *against* in the past. Unable to quite believe she was about to make this case, she said, "But...but that sounds nothing like the Quatro way, as Rug has described it to me. The Quatro way is to look out for the larger group, even if it means endangering one's self."

"The Quatro 'way,' as you describe it, is over and done with it. We left it behind in our Home Systems, where the Assembly of Elders used it to justify their attempts to control every aspect of Quatro life." The Quatro's lips drew back as it talked, to reveal a mouthful of great fangs, which Lisa took as an expression of disgust. "In exchange for our freedom, which we gave up willingly, they promised to feed us. But shortages were many—not just of luxuries but of the basics for life. In exchange for our dignity, they promised us the ability to believe what we wished. And yet they expunged the parts of reality they did not want us to see. They told us we would have peace, even as they spent heavily on war. They told us we would have the future, even as they expected us to make do with the past. Have I told you enough? Have I delivered a sufficient elegy to the Quatro 'way?'"

Lisa opened her mouth, then closed it again. Her captor had just articulated every problem she herself had with the way the Quatro lived, far better than she ever could have.

This is an argument I won't win, especially since I don't believe in my own side.

"The drifts are splintered," the Quatro said. "And we must look out for ourselves." Deliberately, the alien turned and began to pad down the tunnel, away from the jail. "We have not yet decided what is to be done with you," it said as it departed.

With that, the jailor was gone, and only Rug remained outside the cell.

Her eyes met Lisa's, and the pain of being unable to communicate returned. Lisa and Rug had once again become members of two very different species—aliens to each other, in every way. Their drift was broken.

Except, something in Rug's midnight eyes told her she was being foolish. Something in them comforted Lisa, and she felt a smile blossom on her lips.

Rug inclined her head, and with that she padded after the other Quatro.

CHAPTER 33

Simpatico

Jake charged at the first alien mech, which also served to take him out of the second mech's attack vector.

He put everything he had into the attack, and it seemed his target didn't expect such instant decisiveness. It gave way before it, and together they sailed into what remained of a barn, obliterating the one wall still standing.

Landing on top of his opponent, Jake headbutted it, his forehead sprouting a rotating auger as he did.

His aim was to end this fight instantly, so that he only had one opponent to face. But he should have known from his first fight with an alien mech—the one he currently piloted—that this one wouldn't go smoothly, either.

As the auger connected with his enemy's face, that face simply split into two, and the auger hit nothing but the barn floor.

Twin spires shot up from the alien mech's torso, digging into Jake and suspending him over his adversary by several feet.

Dangling there for a moment, he began to panic, and the insects covering his skin multiplied in number and size.

Then, he *inverted*, just as he had in the Belt while fighting Ravagers. Now he faced the barn's ceiling, or at least where the ceiling once had been. That done, he rocketed away, loosening the parts of his mech that had been punctured in order to free himself.

A blast of energy caught him midair, dramatically altering his trajectory and sending him toppling end over end to land in a pond that neighbored the barn.

Use this, the dream-whispers suggested, and Jake instantly knew how. Drawing the water through vents that took shape atop his shoulders, the mech separated the water into hydrogen and oxygen, using the hydrogen to propel itself through the surface.

But Jake continued to rocket through the air well after breaking out of the pond, sketching a steep parabola. At its peak, he used his thrusters to keep him aloft while ordering his arms to become energy cannons.

It took him less than a second to locate his targets on the ground.

There. They were standing next to each other, seeming to stare up at him.

He loosed bolt after white-hot energy bolt at them, forcing them to scurry across the terrain like mice.

That emboldened Jake, and he altered the angle of his thrusters while sprouting new ones, the result being that he screamed toward his opponents, intent on ripping them both apart.

That turned out to be a mistake. The mechs turned as one, aligning their forearms, both of them pointing at Jake.

Then, the alien mechs did something unexpected. Their forearms melded together—one mech's right arm joining with the other's left—to become a single, massive energy cannon.

That cannon unleashed an immense blast of energy at Jake, scoring a direct hit.

After that, all was nothingness. Dim impressions of...something...reached him through the void he inhabited, but they didn't seem to affect him. Not really.

Whatever those vague sensations signified, whatever events they provided an outline for, they were happening to someone else.

Jake was apart from it all, a spectator, and one who wasn't paying very much attention.

Then, gradually, he returned to consciousness—or at least, the facsimile of consciousness offered by the mech dream.

The darkness began to lighten, and he became aware of great pain, as well as the insects that dug into his flesh, bloodying him, gnawing on his organs.

The alien mechs had set him against the base of the spire atop which perched the artificial sun, and the way they pummeled him against that black obelisk without breaking it was a testament to its exquisite engineering, not to mention the nanocarbons that had been used in its construction.

Jake's head lolled down, and he became aware of the rough shape his own mech was now in. The front of his torso was splayed open in several places, and one of the enemy mechs continued to slam its fists into him while the other cut him with the blades its hands had become.

Submit to me, Jake's mech whispered to him. *Let us make our union permanent, so that we might become simpatico and gain the power to vanquish these interlopers.*

"Submit..." Jake muttered.

It was tempting. He wasn't sure what the mech was proposing, exactly, except that it would almost certainly cost him, probably dearly.

But if sacrificing himself was what it took to save Hub...to protect Sue Anne...

Embrace destiny and become one with this conduit to the void and to the universe, to the true oneness, yes, this will take us to heights greater than we could ever achieve alone. Good, we must seek the good, and the path to good is through unification. Our union is that which nullifies, that which makes the same, but to nullify we must unify and to unify we must—

"Sue Anne," Jake said, speaking with conviction, now.

Did Sue Anne want her *brother* to return to her, or did she want whatever he'd turn into after accepting the alien mech's proposal?

Would it even be worth surviving if survival meant living on as whatever creature he'd need to become?

Jake decided it wasn't worth it, and that he would sooner die.

Looking down at himself again, he watched as the blades wielded by one of the enemy mechs laid him open completely. A final cut revealed the cocoon where Jake's dreaming form was curled, exposing it to the air, as well as to the mech's sword.

That sword darted forward, and in that instant, which seemed to stretch on for an eternity, Jake decided that death was also an unacceptable outcome. He needed to return to his sister.

A blade sprang from his mech's ravaged stomach to parry his enemy's thrust, and Jake's left arm became a cannon which swung up to blast the mech who'd been pummeling him.

That only succeeded in driving the mech back a couple of meters, but it gave Jake enough space to do what needed to be done.

He seized the mech who'd nearly killed him, digging razor-sharp metal claws into its front. Then, Jake rocketed upward, carrying his adversary along for the ride.

As he flew, up and away from the central spire, he command-ed the front of his mech to continue knitting back together, in-creasing the shielding that protected his human frame.

That was good, because his captive continued to employ its blades in a desperate attempt to escape.

It would not escape. As they drew level with the artificial sun in the comet's center, Jake threw the mech toward it, blasting it with energy to ensure it didn't alter its own trajectory in time.

Jake had made sure to line himself up with the landing bay before tossing the mech, and as he fired at his enemy, he also thrust toward the airlock, sending it the command to open for him ahead of time.

The mech collided with the artificial sun as Jake passed through the hatch. A blinding explosion erupted, spreading rap-idly outward, and Jake commanded the inner airlock door to close while rocketing straight through the outer one, tearing it from its casing.

He didn't stop, instead using his momentum combined with the mech's thrusters to rip through the closed outer airlock.

Jetting away through space as fast as he could, he patched the visual sensor feed from his feet through to his HUD so that he could watch the entire comet rupture, great gouts of flame flickering all across its surface.

The entire edifice became a ball of white light before winking out to reveal the void beyond. Jake's implant tracked the trajectories of thousands of pieces of shrapnel, but he was already over a thousand kilometers away, and none would hit him.

CHAPTER 34

Sea of Blades

The hours crept by inside their rocky prison, and Lisa dreaded the idea that she would have to attempt sleep on the jagged, uneven cave floor.

This far underground, her implant's signal was blocked, and so there was no hope of calling for help. She also had no way of checking on Andy, and that upset her just as much.

Their guns had been taken, but their jumpsuits had lights, and they used those to suffuse the cell with a uniform blue murk.

Looking around the cell, Lisa's chest ached to think of how many good people she'd lost since first forming her militia back on Alex. She'd lost many Quatro, too, but it wasn't until now that the alien soldiers were gone that Lisa realized how few humans remained.

The fight to escape Habitat 2 had taken all but nine humans, and now they'd lost Rodney Vickers and Beatie Anderson too. With Bob O'Toole and Andy back with the Quatro drift near the space elevator, that left only four militia members inside the cave with her.

Something creaked near the mouth of their cave-cell, and Lisa whipped around to see a Quatro standing behind the bars.

When she crept closer, the lights of her suit revealed that it was Rug.

"What are you doing?" Lisa hissed, but of course the Quatro couldn't answer.

Instead, the alien held her stare for a long time, and Lisa got the impression she was trying to communicate something.

At last, she walked backward into the cell, picking her steps carefully across the uneven rock floor.

Only then did Rug act. As she retreated down the cave a little, the creaking sound from before continued, followed by a resonant groaning. Next, the bars were ripped from their rock frame by an unseen force to slam against the opposite wall of the tunnel.

Lisa motioned for the others to follow her out.

Looks like I won't have to sleep on those awful rocks after all.

"Good job," Lisa whispered as she neared Rug, throwing her arms around the Quatro's neck.

But Rug wasn't out of surprises. Behind her, the militia's guns were stacked, along with their combat knives, grenades, and the other equipment they'd taken with them from the shuttle.

"Rug...how did you...?"

But the alien turned, walked down the tunnel toward the exit, and glanced back at them before continuing a little farther. Clearly, she wanted Lisa and the others to follow.

They collected their weapons, and Lisa stowed as many grenades around her person as she could fit. Once they'd given their guns a once-over, they crept after Rug, weapons at the ready.

It didn't take long to figure out what had given Rug the opportunity to spring them from their prison. A Gatherer sprang out of the darkness at the Quatro, and she batted it out of the air to explode against the tunnel wall.

With that, the Quatro shot a meaningful look back at Lisa.

"Rug, look out!" Lisa said, pointing.

Without the translator, Rug couldn't understand Lisa's words, but the panicked tone and the gesture seemed sufficient to convey her meaning.

The Quatro turned to behold what Lisa had seen: a host of Gatherers, stretching into the darkness, advancing on their position. A sea of wicked blades writhed at the end of steely tendrils.

Lisa opened fire.

CHAPTER 35

The Altar of Expansion

Lisa couldn't deliver orders to Rug, and so she had to structure her troop movements around the Quatro, with the hope that she knew enough about squad tactics to complement Lisa's efforts rather than hinder them.

"Spread out, two to each side of Rug," she barked, putting two rounds into a Gatherer, which didn't seem to have much effect.

"Rug will take point, but *do not* use her as cover. Instead, provide each other with covering fire, and use Rug as an anchor for your formation."

Three of the soldiers responded with "Yes, ma'am," though Tessa only offered a curt nod.

During their first battle with the Gatherers, Lisa had developed a hunch about their structure. Based on the varying effects her bullets had had then, she'd begun to suspect they were weaker on top than they were from any of their sides—which made sense. Their forward and side carapaces had to be extra-hard, for clearing obstructions as efficiently as they did.

But the tunnel grew narrower, and with her five soldiers spread out in a single rank, Lisa was having difficulty getting many shots in around them.

Though the tunnel was narrow, the ceiling hung pretty far overhead...

Lisa tapped Rug's haunches with the butt of her SL-17's handle.

The Quatro glanced back at her, and Lisa gestured at the ground in a lowering motion.

After a few seconds, during which Lisa was pretty sure Rug's expression was some version of *Are you really asking me to do this*, the Quatro dropped to her stomach, allowing Lisa to clamber onto her back.

She quickly shimmied to the front, near the Quatro's neck, and grabbed a tuft of fur to stabilize herself. The effort caused her shoulder wound to send shooting pain throughout her torso, but she ignored it.

Briefly, she was reminded of riding behind Andy on his hoverbike while gunning down Daybreak goons. She leveled her assault rifle at one of the Gatherers.

Success. Instead of absorbing two clips' worth of bullets before it popped, the Gatherer fragmented after a short burst.

She shifted her muzzle toward another target, then squeezed off another short burst. This time, it took two of them.

By the time she'd neutralized a third, and then a fourth, Lisa had realized that her shots had a greater effect the closer to the center she placed them.

Good. Maybe now we won't go through our entire supply of ammo only to take out a dozen Gatherers.

Well, their supplies weren't quite that constricted, but they were far from unlimited, either.

"Shoot for the very center of each Gatherer's top," she yelled over the tumult of gunfire and the metallic *clanging* of the robots. "It takes a lot less to make 'em pop, that way."

Lisa wondered how many times she could work the phrase "make 'em pop" into conversation today. She liked saying it.

The tide of Gatherers seemed never-ending, but with their improved targeting, the six militia soldiers managed to keep them at bay.

Then, from a side tunnel up ahead, two Quatro—also soldiers of Lisa's militia—came charging through the Gatherers, ignoring the blades that stabbed and smacked at them to trample the robots with their sheer weight.

The Quatro's near-kamikaze run instantly changed the battle, turning it into a rout. It also taught Lisa that the Gatherers were capable of fear, or at least of some manner of self-preservation instinct:

The robots retreated.

The two Quatro, Nail and Fan, were bleeding from dozens of wounds, with scarlet streaming down their heaving flanks.

"That was very brave," Lisa told them. "Thank you." But Nail's translator had also been taken, and Fan hadn't had one since before his drift was stranded on Eresos. Both Quatro only stared at Lisa, their expressions unchanging.

Shrugging, Lisa pushed down the tunnel, her newly bolstered squad backing her up close behind.

Without warning, the tunnel opened up into an enormous cavern, where the floor sloped steeply toward the center, though with wide platforms of level rock here and there.

Campfires dotted the gloom, and upwards of two hundred Quatro were locked in furious combat with what seemed like ten times their number in Gatherers.

The moment Lisa entered, one of the battling Quatro was forced back into one of the fires, and its shrieks echoed off the walls.

Lisa and her companions joined the fight without hesitation, hitting an exposed Gatherer flank hard.

It took the better part of an hour, and a lot of Quatro were slain, but at last they achieved victory against the invaders.

Lisa mourned the felled Quatro, but she also gave silent thanks that no one else from her militia had been killed. She doubted she could have taken that, today.

Shortly after the last Gatherer fell, Lisa came face to face with the Quatro who'd spoken with her through her cell's bars.

"We thank you for your assistance in protecting our home, two-legs," the Quatro said, sounding grudging.

"You're welcome," Lisa said, crossing her arms. "Are you going to ask us to surrender our firearms and return to jail, now?"

The Quatro had no answer for that, it seemed.

"May I borrow the translator? I would address your people." Lisa held out her hand.

Another long silence passed.

At last, the translator became unfastened, without any visible action from the Quatro. It clattered to the rock floor. The Quatro's eyes never left Lisa's.

She stepped forward and picked it up, fastening it around her own neck, though of course the translator drooped far down her chest. Her neck was somewhat thinner than a Quatro's.

Casting her gaze at the host of Quatro assembled before her, Lisa said, "I come from Alex, where I had a fairly cushy job with Darkstream. If you haven't heard of them, they're the ones currently slaughtering Quatro in droves to the west of here."

A long silence settled in after those words, too, and she let it, praying that the implications of her words were also settling in.

You Quatro carry nearly as much blame for those deaths as humans do.

But she didn't say that, not yet, and she hoped she wouldn't have to. "I was on a promising career track with Darkstream. My future was bright. My job was easy, too—I thought it was hard, but it was incredibly easy, and I could have phoned it in for the rest of my life while making piles of credits." She glanced at Tessa, then, before returning her gaze to the Quatro.

"I abandoned that career," Lisa went on, "when I realized how dangerous Darkstream is to the people living in this system. Both human *and* Quatro. They're bent on constant expansion, and they're willing to sacrifice the happiness and prosperity of regular people on the altar of that expansion.

"I sacrificed my future because I didn't want to be a part of the death machine they've created. Now, I've devoted myself to stopping that machine. If you consider it a worthy pursuit to prevent the suffering and death of thousands more innocent humans and Quatro, then I hope you'll join me in my fight."

Lisa unfastened the translator, held out her hand with her fingers downward, and let the device drop onto the cave floor. With that, she walked away.

Suddenly, she realized what she'd just argued for: self-sacrifice for the good of the group. And when she thought about it, that was exactly what she'd been doing ever since turning against Darkstream back on Alex.

All right, she thought. *All right. In certain, very select cases, it's the right thing to do. But only very seldom.*

And anyway, the Quatro tended to take the principle *way* too far.

Lisa glanced over her shoulder at the aliens gathered in the cavern, who'd begun to murmur among themselves in their strange language, which reminded her of both purring and growling at the same time.

I wonder whether I convinced them.

CHAPTER 36

Scratching an Itch

The drift that had captured Lisa and her companions deliberated for a long time, and without access to her translator, Rug wasn't able to fill Lisa in on the proceedings.

All the Quatro could do was stare at her meaningfully, except her expressions didn't actually mean anything to Lisa, because they belonged to an alien whose body language she was still a long way from deciphering, despite their close friendship.

At last, the Quatro stepped forward who'd spoken to her through the bars of her former cell—and possibly her future cell, depending on what was about to happen.

The approaching Quatro appeared to be the leader of this drift. Lisa knew the Quatro weren't supposed to have leaders, but apparently they'd abandoned the "Quatro way," so maybe that meant they did other things differently, too.

"Your words have moved us," the Quatro said when it neared. "Not only to join your fight, but to send runners to the other drifts in this area, who until now have shared our attitude toward the unrest in the west. Hopefully, if our messengers convey your words as effectively as you spoke them, we can sway them, too."

"Hopefully," Tessa said, then stalked off.

Grimacing, Lisa thanked the Quatro and then ran after the white-haired woman.

"Tessa. Wait."

"Why?" Tessa said without turning or slowing. "You've achieved everything you set out to achieve, using everything I've taught you. What more do we have to say to each other?"

"Will you stop?" Lisa said, her voice coming out sharper than she'd meant it to.

Tessa whirled around, her arms crossed, glaring. "Well?"

Stopping a few meters away from Tessa, Lisa studiously kept her hands at her sides, though her impulse was to cross them as well.

"I should hope we have plenty more to say to each other, Tessa. We're friends, and we've been friends for a long time."

"We haven't acted like friends. Not since..."

"Not since I learned yet another secret about you?"

Tessa's head jerked. "What do you mean, *another*—"

"I mean that we're *supposed* to be friends, close friends, and yet you failed to tell me two things that are probably among the most important facts about you. Back in Habitat 2, I learned you worked for Three Points, and I overlooked that you kept that from me, even though we'd spent so much time together. And when we arrived on Eresos, I learned that you helped Darkstream frame the Quatro as ruthless killers. It's not the fact that you did that which bothers me, Tessa—the past is the past, and I understand that you've changed over the last twenty years. It's the fact that, after everything we've gone through together...almost dying on Alex, imprisoned by aliens we didn't even know were there, retaking Habitat 2 from Daybreak, defeating Darkstream to escape to Eresos...even after all that, it still took Gabriel *Roach* for me to learn the truth about you."

Tessa's face had turned scarlet, and Lisa felt sure she was about to explode. If Tessa did that, she wasn't sure they could go on being friends, no matter how much Lisa liked her.

If, after I bare my heart to her, she lambastes me...

But Tessa didn't do that. Instead, she took several deep breaths, and gradually, the color drained from her face, restoring it to what Lisa was pretty sure was her regular color—it was difficult to tell in the gloom of the tunnel.

"You're right, Lisa," the older woman said at last. "That's hard for me to say, because I'm not using to being wrong. I'm used to being surrounded by idiots. But...you're right. And I'm sorry."

Lisa stepped forward to embrace her friend, and Tessa allowed it, which she also hadn't expected.

They drew apart, and Lisa cast her eyes down at the tunnel floor. "I haven't behaved very well, either," she said. "The strain of command has been getting to me, and I've been taking it out on you. That wasn't right, no matter how upset I was with you. I'm sorry, too."

"Hey," Tessa said, placing a hand on her shoulder. "We forgive each other. Now let's put it behind us and go put down

Darkstream. That's an itch I've been waiting a *long* time to scratch."

A smile crept over Lisa's face. "You got it."

CHAPTER 37

Data Dump

Ash sifted through the data dump DuGalle had sent her, using a panel in the upper left of her vision to process its contents as best she could.

Unfortunately, most of her attention was demanded by tracking Roach and navigating through the forest; taking care not to barrel into a tree big enough to repel her MIMAS.

Roach, it seemed, didn't have that problem. Whereas before, when he'd run alongside Oneiri through the woods, he'd chosen his path with care, now it seemed erratic.

They found several thick trees that were little more than cracked-off stumps, with the rest of the tree obliterated. The juggernaut that was the alien mech was powerful enough that nothing seemed able to stop it.

What information Ash's fragmented attention did allow her to glean from DuGalle's transfer disturbed her deeply.

When she'd seen enough, she used her implant to contact Bronson, which she'd been putting off.

"Sweeney," he said as he appeared beside her, darting through the trees. "What do you have for me?"

What do *I have for you, Bronson?* It was a fine question, and it would be some time before she fully developed the answer.

"Roach betrayed us," she said. "He murdered Richaud, in the middle of a battle."

"God. Seriously?" Bronson did a good job of feigning shock and distress as he ran alongside her in the dream, but Ash knew that any negative reaction he had to the news would be limited to how it would look on the company's ledger.

"Yes, Captain. Really."

"Well, where's Roach now?"

"En route to the nearest village, it seems. We're following him."

"Good. Definitely keep doing that." Bronson palmed something from his cheek. "He has to be stopped. This could easily turn into a PR disaster if we don't deal with it early."

"Not to mention the lives that will likely be lost."

"Yes, another tragedy, to be sure." Bronson's likeness seemed distracted, as though the actual Bronson was focusing on something else while he spoke with Ash. "Two reserve battalions are already in the area, and I'm sending them to rendezvous with you at...River Rock, I'm guessing? Seems to make sense, judging by your trajectory, which will take you out of the Glades and toward the edge of the Barrens. Is River Rock right, Sweeney?"

"That's the one."

"Perfect. I'd advise against engaging until they've joined you."

"And what do you plan to do in the meantime, sir?"

"Huh?" Bronson blinked up at her. "Me? I'm working on a way to beat the machines, Sweeney. There have been a dozen more reports from all over the region of Gatherers attacking residents. If this becomes a pattern, we're going to have a real Charlie Foxtrot on our hands."

"Yeah." Ash paused to consider what her next words should be.

"Will that be all, Seaman?"

"Well, it looks like Red Company has disbanded."

"That's welcome news. I needed that. How'd you come across it?"

"I spoke to their leader. He was at Peppertree, during the Quatro attack. He..." Ash drew a breath.

"Something on your mind, Sweeney?"

"Sir, he told me that Darkstream started the war with the Quatro. He said we paid Red Company to put on company uniforms and attack them, and afterward, we paid them to deliver arms to the aliens."

"Oh? Well, I wouldn't know anything about that. Must have been another department."

Abruptly, Ash stopped running to stare at Bronson.

His simulacrum stopped too, smiling up at her. "That was a joke, Sweeney. Obviously I don't know about it, because it didn't happen."

She shook her head, not sure what to think, or to say. At last, she found words: "He gave me documents to back up what he said."

"Then they're forged. Darkstream wouldn't do something like that, Sweeney. You know that."

Ash studied Bronson's face. Could he really be that masterful at lying? Or could the documents actually have been forged? Certainly, the technology existed to do that, but a data dump this size would have taken weeks of nonstop work to concoct. She supposed it was possible, but Red Company had had limited resources as it was, and she wasn't sure they'd have had access to the sophisticated tech required to forge video and audio. Besides, if they'd wanted to damage Darkstream's reputation, a single, well-executed video would have sufficed. The sheer number of documents DuGalle had given her spoke of truth.

"Are we going to have a problem, here, Sweeney?" Bronson said, the mirth draining from his voice.

She returned his gaze, her mind racing. Bronson was hailed as a hero throughout the Steele System. He was the man who'd bested the authoritarian Captain Keyes; the man who'd led a battle group of rogue UHF warships away from the Milky Way's tyrannical Commonwealth; and also the one who'd secured Darkstream's transition into this galaxy.

Bronson was also the man who'd conquered Eresos for use by Darkstream colonists.

But maybe the popular portrayal had Bronson exactly backward. Maybe he'd accomplished everything through manipulation instead of the bravery and sacrifice everyone attributed to him. The idea seemed as unlikely a proposition as DuGalle's entire data dump being fake, but maybe that was only because Bronson commanded such respect.

In one sense, the idea he's a snake is much, much simpler.

"Sweeney?"

"We don't have a problem, Captain. I'll lead Oneiri on to River Rock. But we'd better get going." She gestured with a giant metal hand at the path ahead, where the rest of Oneiri had stopped to peer back at her. "Otherwise, we'll risk losing Roach's trail."

"You do that," Bronson said, and his eyes were narrowed as he flickered out of existence.

CHAPTER 38

The Debt

Jake knew the physics checked out: with the distances involved, blowing up Comet Three's artificial sun should not have negatively affected the environments inside the surrounding comets. Even if the radiation had reached them, the thirty meters of soil would have been more than enough to soak it up.

Even so, he still insisted that Pichenko check the comet's radiation levels. The last thing his conscience needed was the slimmest chance he'd exposed his sister to even more radiation, let alone his mother and the rest of Comet Four's inhabitants.

When the tests came back normal, he breathed a small sigh of relief.

But that was hardly the only thing bothering him.

The fight with the alien mechs played over and over again in his mind, both while sleeping and awake.

It wasn't the combat itself that got to him most, though that had come pretty close to ending him.

No, the most disturbing thing was the part he still had to contend with, on an ongoing basis: the dark whispers the mech continued to feed his mind whenever he was inside it.

He had no one he could talk to about it; no one who would understand the torment, the constant *darkness* involved with being inside the mech.

The knowledge that if he was going to protect his family and his friends through whatever was happening to the Steele System, he would *need* the mech...

It made his throat clench whenever he thought about it.

He couldn't talk to his mother about it. She would tell him to stop using it, end-of-conversation. Jake knew that wasn't an option, but for Brianne Price, even that wouldn't matter. The safety of her children was paramount, and every other consideration was subordinate to it.

Neither could he talk about it to his father. Aside from the ten-minute delay their conversation would suffer from, telling Peter would only cause him to worry more than he already did, and he worried *a lot.*

Who could understand the unending torment Jake endured? Who could relate to the awareness that the torment might never end—that moving forward meant contending with it, day after day, possibly for the rest of his life?

Then, as he walked alone through the fields of Comet Four, which were greening once again, the answer came to him:

Sue Anne. Sue Anne would understand.

But no. He couldn't possibly discuss this with his sister. She had enough darkness in her life to grapple with.

And yet...he'd had nothing to talk to her about before. Nothing had seemed real enough.

This was certainly real.

And if he wanted to feel comfortable talking to his sister...wanted to show that, on some abstract level, he could relate to her situation...

He knew it was awful. But he went to her all the same.

His mother and his sister were still at Pichenko's house, even though they'd discovered that many other Comet Four homes were vacant as well.

Pichenko had grimaced when Jake had raised the specter of his family moving into one of them. "Pardon me if this is callous, Jake, but the last thing your family needs is to stay in a home belonging to the recently deceased. It's the last thing I need, for that matter. No. They must remain in mine. I am more than comfortable in the Council Chambers."

Jake nodded at his mother when he entered the house, and she glanced up from some reading, smiling halfheartedly before returning to it.

He smiled back, hoping his expression looked more genuine than hers, and he continued through the house...to the sick room.

When he opened the door, he found his sister asleep, and he settled into the rocking chair beside her bed as silently as he could.

Even so, the chair creaked, and Sue Anne's eyes fluttered open. They found him.

"Jake?" she rasped.

There was a note of surprise in her voice, and that killed him. He knew it belonged there, though. He'd been avoiding this room, spending much longer periods out searching the other comets for survivors than he should reasonably have expected of himself, of which his mother continually reminded him.

"Hi, Sue Anne," he said.

"Something's bothering you. Isn't it? Something big."

He raised his eyebrows. "How can you tell?"

"When you spend months at a time in bed, you get really good at reading the people who visit you."

"That makes sense," he said, and then he sighed. "I...I haven't visited you. Not nearly enough. I'm sorry."

"Don't be. I understand."

Jake returned her gaze, and he could see that she did understand—fully. That made it even worse.

"Tell me what's bothering you," she said.

"It's that, uh, that *thing* I pilot." For some reason, saying the words 'alien mech' out loud felt a little ridiculous. "It's getting to me. To be honest, it scares me."

Sue Anne shook her head a little against the pillow, and even that seemed to require a tremendous effort. "Why?"

"It keeps trying to...to *tempt* me."

"It's sentient?"

"I don't know. Maybe. It's *something*. Possessed, maybe." He laughed, though he wasn't sure he was joking. "It whispers to me. Keeps asking me to *join* with it. I don't know what it means by that, exactly, but it seems like a bad idea. On the other hand, I keep getting this idea that if I give in, I'll become even better equipped to fight the things that attacked Hub. And maybe, if I'm quick enough, I can help save Eresos from them, too."

"You must not give in, Jake."

Studying her gaunt face, he said, "Why do you say that? What could you possibly know about it?"

"I know that you just said it's a bad idea. You've spent a long time inside it, by now. You have a lot of experience with that thing, and you're my brother, and I trust your judgment."

He nodded. "Thanks. But, Sue Anne...I'm not sure how much longer I can hold out against it."

"*Listen to me,*" Sue Anne hissed, and genuine anger filled her voice. "Are you listening, Jake?"

"Yes...yes. I'm listening."

"Good. Because what I'm about to say is *very* important. For most of my life, I've dealt with more pain than you can imagine. I don't care what Darkstream did to you in training. I don't care what you've encountered in battle. All I have to do is take one look at you to tell that you haven't encountered a fraction of the pain that I have, on a daily basis, for years and years and years. Are you following me?"

"Yes," he whispered, and his voice was barely audible, even to him.

"Good. Then I hope you'll believe me when I tell you that the pain I've experienced makes life *not worth living.*"

"Sue Anne—"

"Shut up. I'm not kidding. It's not worth it, to live like this. I would honestly rather be dead. So, why do I cling to life, when I could have stopped fighting at any second? When I could have let my sickness take me and it all would have ended?"

Sue Anne's eyes held his gaze as they burned with more energy than he would have thought possible. He didn't dare speak.

"Jake, I clung to life because I could see how important it was to mom, to dad, and to *you* that I go on living. I saw how hard you all worked on the fantasy that you could somehow save me from this dragon that has been ravaging my body since I was five. I did it for you, Jake. For *you*." If Sue Anne's illness hadn't dramatically diminished her voice, she would have been shouting, now.

"So when you hear that thing's voice calling to you, beckoning to you to give in, here's what I want you to do. I want you to remember me, fighting to live, despite how badly I wanted to die. I want you to remember how much you owe me. How deeply in debt you are to me—a debt you can never, *ever* repay, except by continuing to resist that voice, forever."

Jake couldn't answer, because he was weeping, now, and the tears showed no sign of stopping. He sobbed so hard that speech wasn't an option.

At last, after a long, long time, he did manage to utter two syllables.

"*Thank you.*"

CHAPTER 39

Silence

The next day, Jake called his father, despite how difficult the communications delay rendered conversation.

That didn't matter, not really. Because Jake only had one thing to say of any importance:

"Come home, Dad. It's time for you to come home."

And he did. A day later, Peter stepped out of the airlock, and Jake and his mother were there to greet him.

His parents exchanged thin, tight smiles, and together the three of them walked to Councilman Pichenko's house.

"Did you call your comet hoppers to come?" Jake asked.

His father nodded. "And I put out the call to other development outfits. A few of them resisted, but after I showed them the footage, most agreed."

"Good."

In addition to the ships used to develop comets, the residents of Hub would also employ every shuttle in the city-settlement that still functioned, and a request had been put out to the entire Steele System: anyone with a spacecraft at their disposal was asked to come to Hub and help with the evacuation.

It was doubtful any of the eleven warships that had accompanied Darkstream to the Steele System would come to Hub's rescue. A scant handful of those were devoted to patrolling the space between the Belt and the inner system, but Darkstream used most of them as passenger and cargo ships, and they rarely stayed in one place for long. Jake doubted they'd divert from their courses—not even to help the thousands of refugees from Hub.

Across all seven comets, Jake had found nine thousand survivors, mostly located in Comet Two. Though the population of Hub had varied somewhat, it had once averaged around a hundred thousand—over ten times the number of people who were left.

They arrived at Pichenko's house, and Brianne paused briefly before opening the front door, offering Peter a smile that was a little warmer than earlier.

Then they all entered, making their way to the sick room, where Peter Price reunited with his daughter at long last.

She wasn't able to lift herself from the bed even an inch, and Peter had to gently slide his arms underneath her so they could embrace.

After that, the conversation was sparse, but it didn't seem to matter. Sue Anne looked truly happy, and that did matter.

After less than an hour, they left Sue Anne's room, unwilling to deprive her of the rest she so badly needed. She would need as much energy as she could muster for the journey into the inner system.

But as it happened, she would never make that journey.

Before bed, Jake slipped inside Sue Anne's room to kiss her goodnight. He tiptoed across the room, not wanting to wake her.

The military had taught him to interpret sense-data quickly, and he instantly noted the silence, where once there had been the steady beep-beep-beep of the heart monitor.

He traced the cord and found that Sue Anne had disconnected it from herself—she must not have wanted to disturb them with its shrill and steady keening.

When Jake touched her forehead, there was still some warmth there.

He sat on the edge of the rocking chair, holding Sue Anne's limp, cooling hand. And for the second time in as many days, he cried.

CHAPTER 40

River Rock Redux

After receiving Bronson's orders, Oneiri slowed their pace toward River Rock. They were meant to reunite with the two reserve battalions, after all, and although both were in the area, they moved much slower than the **MIMAS** mechs.

As she picked her way through the woods, Ash struggled with the implications of the data dump DuGalle had given her.

If it truly held water—and a big part of her screamed that it must—then Darkstream had orchestrated the war with the Quatro from the outset. They'd launched an unprovoked attack against the aliens, with the sole intention of drawing them into a prolonged conflict and increasing company profits.

But a Quatro killed Jess.

How could she reconcile her sister's death with the possibility that the Quatro had never wanted this war in the first place? That their attack on Ash's home had been in response to repeated attacks on their own?

At last, she couldn't take it anymore, and she forwarded the data dump to the other members of Oneiri Team.

"Fake," Henrietta said after a cursory glance.

"Are you kidding me?" Ash said. "You can't have looked at more than one or two of the documents."

"The tech for doctoring basically anything has been around for ages. Right, Spirit?"

Haltingly, Marco nodded as he dodged around a particularly large tree. "Well, yes..."

"See? Case closed. Who are you going to trust, Steam? Red Company, or the company that made us *mech pilots?*"

Ash paused for several seconds, collecting her thoughts. She'd been reasoning this out for hours, but now that Henrietta was actually confronting her about it, her arguments had promptly fled.

"I don't know, Razor," she finally said. "It seems like it would have taken a hell of a lot of effort for Red Company to forge all these documents. Did they even have the resources to do it? I mean, they disbanded because they *lack* resources, didn't they?"

"They're conniving bastards," Henrietta said. "They would have found a way. And as for them 'disbanding,' I don't trust that for a second. Sure, they *said* they're disbanding. But what better way would there be for them to catch us off-guard?"

Realizing she needed more time to puzzle over it, Ash fell back into her own thoughts. Henrietta spoke so plainly, with such conviction, that it was difficult to argue with her. The confident way she talked made Ash feel like everything Henrietta said should have been self-evident, and like everything Ash thought was silly.

At last, they joined with the Venomous Vipers and the Pied Pipers. This time, Ash barely batted an eyelash at the moronic names Darkstream's reserve battalions inevitably took for themselves.

The force they brought to bear was no joke, however: eight tanks, five mortar teams, forty snipers, and ten platoons' worth of infantry would give Roach a hard time no matter how powerful he was now.

Darkstream was clearly intent on putting Gabriel Roach down like the rabid dog he'd become.

But when they rolled into River Rock, Roach was nowhere to be seen.

In his place, hundreds of corpses littered the village, so thickly that patches of visible ground were rare. The bodies had already begun to attract insects, which briefly vacated their meals as the Darkstream soldiers passed before lighting upon them once more.

There weren't only human bodies—there were Quatro bodies among the dead as well, dwarfing their human counterparts. And though Ash wasn't certain, she would have bet that the dead Quatro were the same ones Oneiri had fought in both Cordage and Peppertree.

Most of the structures were also obliterated, though Ash got the impression that not all of the damage had been done recently. Some of it looked like it had been in the middle of getting repaired when it had been ripped apart once more.

Sure enough, when she consulted the system net it told her that River Rock had already suffered from one attack, consisting of six Quatro led by a quad.

Something moved amidst the corpses, and in an instant dozens of guns were trained on it.

It was a human corpse, bouncing up and down—once, twice, three times.

At last, it fell out of the way, and a hatch opened beneath it, which must have led directly into the ground.

An elderly man emerged out of the hatch, both wavering hands held high in the air.

"Who are you?" Ash demanded.

"Billy Overton." He nodded, ever so slightly, at the hatch he'd just vacated. "This here's my shelter. Paid tens of thousands of credits for it, and let me tell you, it was worth every penny."

Ash exchanged looks with Beth. Then she turned back to the old man. "What happened here?"

"Bunch of Quatro showed up, led by two in those four-legged mechs. Then, a two-legged mech showed up—alien-looking one, very same one as saved this village a couple weeks ago, far as I can tell. Except, this time he joined the Quatro in their killing. They didn't just kill humans, neither. The Quatro mechs turned on their own kind. I saw it. I watched it all from down there." He nodded again toward the hatch he'd emerged from.

Turning to scan the soldiers that circled them, Ash spotted Commander Janessa Okar, who'd been placed in command of both battalions.

"Commander, would it be possible to arrange a shuttle to evacuate Mr. Overton?"

Okar nodded. "Of course."

Turning to the three **MIMAS** pilots that remained under her command, Ash said, "We can cover ground the fastest. Spread out and look for signs of where Roach might be headed next."

"What will you do?" Henrietta said, and Ash's gaze snapped onto the face of Henrietta's mech. The somewhat impertinent question reminded her of the one she'd asked Bronson just hours ago.

"I'm going to download satellite photos and study them."

Henrietta made a sound that was difficult to decipher, and with that, the other three mechs entered the woods, in three separate directions.

Nearby, Overton was arguing vehemently with the soldier trying to escort him to the shuttle's landing zone.

"I got my shelter," Overton said, gnarled hands planted firmly on his hips. "It's got me this far. Plenty of food, and plenty of security!"

"Sir, please—"

"I'm not going with you. And that's that."

CHAPTER 41

We Stick Together

An hour of searching by Henrietta, Marco, and Beth brought no results, and finally, Commander Okar ordered one of her battalions to join the search as well.

Ash hadn't wanted to suggest that outright, since she still wasn't sure how their delicate division of power was supposed to work. But she'd certainly hinted at it pretty overtly, and she was glad when Okar finally arrived at the decision.

Forty more minutes of searching yielded a trail, which Ash suspected had gone pretty cold by now.

Nevertheless, it was all they had, and they continued along it. It pointed directly at Vanguard, the largest settlement that bordered the Barrens. They'd begun building walls at Vanguard, though construction had halted once it had become known walls were now useless in defending against the Quatro. Either way, the town was well on its way to becoming Eresos' third true city.

That was, if everything didn't fall completely to pieces before then.

Fifteen minutes into following the trail they'd found, they received an emergency bulletin that Vanguard was indeed under attack by three alien mechs—one biped and two quadrupeds.

It seemed beyond likely that it was Roach, apparently aligned now with the Quatro mechs.

The Darkstream force doubled its speed, which came as a tremendous relief to Ash. Under the best of circumstances, the reserve battalions came nowhere near to matching the MIMAS mechs for speed, but at least, now that they'd quickened their pace, they might have beaten a glacier in a race.

Although, maybe they'd have to increase their speed just a little more to do that.

At last, they neared Vanguard, and Okar began handing down orders with a crispness and precision that Ash had to admire.

Partly for defensive reasons, and partly because of the direct access it granted the town to Gatherers laden with resources, Vanguard had been built in a cleft formed by two sheer, towering cliffs. Those cliffs embraced the town like a lover, exposing less than half of her to the cruel world.

Even the terrain that led to Vanguard was hilly; uneven. That made the town's location enviable, from a defensive perspective. At least, it should have.

Despite that the alien mechs were already rampaging through the town's streets, Okar showed restraint that was as admirable as much as it was likely difficult.

Before anything else, the commander spread the Darkstream reserve battalions out over the hills, in a wide arc that surrounded the part of the town not covered by the cliffs.

Only then did she send in Oneiri to draw the enemy out.

If she was being honest, Ash didn't like her odds. The MIMAS mechs had already been proven inferior to those of alien make, even though they *had* succeeded in taking down one of the quads.

That had required intensive collaboration, and Oneiri's numbers had been reduced even more since then.

This looks grim.

But her training hadn't taught her to think like that. As a soldier, she was supposed to charge into battle, unhesitating, no matter how daunting the odds. She was supposed to follow orders, even if those orders asked her to face what seemed like near-certain death.

So that was what she did.

And it was also what Marco Gonzalez, Henrietta Jin, and Beth Arkanian did. If none of them made it through today, Ash hoped that they would at least be remembered for the way they unflinchingly followed the order that sent them to their deaths.

As it happened, they did not need to enter Vanguard. Just as they neared the outskirts, Roach emerged from behind one of the outer structures—a warehouse, from the looks of it.

Flanking him were the two Quatro mechs that Billy Overton had said accompanied him, which reports from Vanguard's beleaguered garrison had confirmed.

The trio of alien mechs galloped across the dry terrain, a great cloud of dust rising behind them.

"Fall back," Ash said. "Let the reserve battalions soften them up."

"You go ahead," Henrietta said. "I'm staying. I already told you—he's mine."

"Razor, no. You know they'll run your MIMAS over. Our mechs are most effective when we're backed up by a variety of units."

"You're right, Steam. That's why you three should retreat. You can have whatever's left of Roach when I'm done with him."

"Roach is currently backed up by two quite powerful quadruped mechs," Marco reminded Henrietta, but she didn't respond.

"*Razor,*" Ash said sharply, and Henrietta glanced back at her. Beyond, Roach and his companions were closing the distance. "If you stay, we all stay. You know that. We're Oneiri Team, and we stick together, damn it."

Henrietta turned back to the oncoming enemies. "Tell that to Roach," she said. "You can do what you want. I'm taking him on."

Heaving a sigh, Ash turned to Marco and Beth. "All right, team. Rockets first. Then autocannons. After that, prepare to engage at close quarters."

Marco tried one more time: "Henrietta..."

"Shut up, Marco."

With that, Oneiri assumed a single rank and began sending missile after missile at the oncoming mechs, which were now shimmering in the heat.

CHAPTER 42

Her New Army

"**I**ncredible," Lisa whispered. "I'm like a general, now, or something."

She stood atop a piece of land that swept up out of the Barrens, affording her a view of the tremendous host that passed before her, causing the earth to tremor.

Her tremendous host.

Either the other Quatro drifts scattered throughout this region held more closely to the "Quatro way" than did the drift that had captured Lisa and her soldiers, or her words really had been persuasive, even when translated into the Quatro language and repeated.

Either way, over a thousand of the aliens had responded to the call, pledging to fight Darkstream in order to liberate their brethren.

More Quatro messengers were remaining behind, to continue searching for and persuading other Quatro drifts. Any they succeeded in recruiting would follow behind the advance force.

Most of the Quatro had never been in their own species' military, and so they were content for Lisa to take the command, since she already led the militia from Alex and had racked up a decent amount of combat experience, at this point.

Not to mention the thorough training she'd received at the hands of the woman whose voice now spoke behind her:

"You did it," Tessa said.

Lisa turned to find the white-haired woman marching up the incline to join her, showing none of her age.

"*We* did it," Lisa said.

"Either way. We actually have a fighting chance against Darkstream, now, especially after we join with the Quatro near the space elevator. And we can finally leak the footage of Darkstream's behavior on Alex. It won't just sink into obscurity—we actually have the teeth to make them pay for their crimes."

Sighing, Lisa nodded slightly. "Maybe. But if Eresos' robots are turning on us...I don't know. There are a lot of Amblers on this planet, Tessa, and a lot of Gatherers. If they all hit us together..."

"Then we'll do something about it. What have I told you? There's no use entertaining anxiety about something that hasn't happened yet. And if it does happen, we'll handle it."

"I hope you're right." Lisa turned to leave the rise and rejoin her forces.

The Eresos Quatro had had their technology stripped away from them by the Meddlers before getting stranded here. But Rug and the others still had their devastating energy weapons, as well as their multipurpose jumpsuits.

Lisa knew from Alex that her implant interfaced well with the Quatro communicators, and now she used that connection to locate Rug in the vast alien throng.

"I'm near the front of the great drift, Lisa Sato. Join me and we shall talk."

Lisa chuckled at the Quatro's grandiose way of talking. "Will do, Rug. I'm coming now."

Even though the Quatro were consciously checking their speed to make sure the humans could catch up, it still took a brisk jog to overtake them in order to catch up to Rug.

Lisa had ordered the shuttles they'd stolen from Darkstream to remain where they were until they received further instructions. It wouldn't do to have them fly into a warzone exposed, and it didn't serve much to have them leapfrog along with their force, either.

She might have waited behind with them and hitched a ride once her force drew close enough to the warzone, where the battle between Darkstream and Quatro still raged, at least according to the system net.

But abandoning her new army immediately after rallying it didn't feel right. A good leader walked alongside her soldiers and shared in their hardship.

Tessa had taught her that.

By the time she reached Rug, the front of the group was just nearing a canyon bracketed by towering cliffs. Lisa thought she remembered seeing it from the shuttle's cockpit as they flew overhead, during the trip to locate the eastern Quatro drifts. If she was right, the canyon continued for almost two kilometers before the cliffs leveled out into more open terrain—or at least, as open as the Barrens ever got.

"How is Andy Miller?" the Quatro asked once Lisa arrived.

"On the mend, from what I hear. He's up and on his feet—well, foot. Apparently the Quatro we left him and Bob with are looking after him. One of them fashioned him a set of crutches using materials from a Gatherer." Lisa had gotten in touch to check on Andy the moment she'd returned to the planet's surface and her implant signal had been restored.

"These are good tidings," Rug said.

As they reached the mouth of the canyon, a rocket left the cliff on their right, sailing through the air to connect with the front ranks of the Quatro army.

Flame licked the dry air, and an explosion rocked the ground while Lisa's heart leapt toward her throat. When the smoke and dust cleared, she saw that three Quatro were down, not moving.

A second rocket came, connecting with another Quatro, this one closer to Lisa and Rug. The missile had been loosed from a hidden cleft somewhere partway up the cliff to the left.

Squinting through the chaos and into the canyon, Lisa saw a battalion of robots who were just now turning a corner and emerging from the cliffs' shadows, the sun glinting off their metal surfaces.

"Fall back!" Lisa screamed, and then she repeated the message over a wide channel.

But most of her force did not have the means to listen over the wide channel, and as disorder took hold over their ranks, with some Quatro surging forward to meet the attackers while others turned to try to flee through the thick alien horde, Lisa began to panic herself.

CHAPTER 43

Vanguard

Roach and his new quad friends dodged around the rockets Oneiri fired at them with ease, changing trajectory and speeding up as needed.

"We need to coordinate," Ash barked over a team-wide channel, though the urgency in her voice wouldn't come through over the subvocalization. "Let's focus on the rightmost Quatro. Spirit, Paste—help me corral it while Razor tries to land a hit."

"I told you," Henrietta shot back. "I'm aiming for Roach."

"Damn it, Razor!" Ash yelled, and she didn't subvocalize this time. "Are you abandoning the entire concept of a military unit operating efficiently together? Have you decided the chain of command doesn't suit you today? Or are you going to actually act like a soldier?"

Henrietta glanced sideways at her, and Ash was sure if she could have seen her face, it would have been glaring.

But when Henrietta turned back toward the enemy, she gave a sullen shrug and ground out, "*Fine.*"

Beth landed a rocket to the Quatro mech's left, forcing it to veer right, and then Marco put one between it and Roach.

That gave it no path but forward, and Ash decided to take the shot. When the quad sped up again, angling slightly left, Henrietta loosed a missile that scored a direct hit.

Beth whooped, but stopped when none of the others joined her.

Any cause for feeling triumphant was short-lived: the explosion dispersed, and the quad emerged from the smoke, virtually unscathed.

"They're getting too close for rockets. Engage rotary auto-cannons and sweep them," Ash ordered.

The others complied, peppering the trio of mechs with armor-piercing rounds.

Even though the high-velocity rounds lent a stutter to the enemy mechs' step, it did not slow them by much. They barreled closer and closer.

"All right," Ash said, her voice tight. "Prepare to extend bayonets."

But when Roach and the two quads were about to close with Oneiri, they split apart—Roach and one quad sprinting past to Oneiri's right while the other quad passed on their left.

"What the hell?" Henrietta growled.

Ash saw instantly what the enemy was doing: by charging straight at the Darkstream reserve battalions, they'd made it hazardous for the MIMAS mechs to continue firing at them, for fear of hitting friendlies.

That meant they only had to contend with the weaker artillery wielded by the soldiers under Janessa Okar's command.

Still, there was a lot of that artillery. A tank scored a direct hit on one of the quads, ripping its shoulder half-off. The metal instantly began to knit itself back together, though, and within seconds it had reformed.

Still, Okar knew what she was doing, and threads of deadly light came from all over the wide arc she'd established—straight at the enemy mechs, whose progress was significantly impeded, now.

There was no avoiding that massive barrage of ordnance, and the trio of mechs could only continue their forward surge.

For a moment—as hundreds of metal fragments were shot off the alien mechs' sides and heavy ordnance continued to hammer their fronts, which had to be doing major damage—Ash dared to hope.

Were the mechs about to go down without inflicting *any* casualties on Darkstream's forces?

But then Roach and the quads reached the Darkstream ranks.

Immediately, most of the shooting dropped off, to avoid friendly fire. The soldiers around the mechs tried to pull away from them to continue shooting, but clearly Roach and the Quatro now considered it *their* turn.

They wouldn't let the Darkstream soldiers get away, keeping close to them instead.

The Quatro mechs charged through the ranks, impaling infantry on twin lances that sprouted downward from their shoulders while firing from batteries of guns that projected from their flanks.

A broadside barrage from a ground unit. Ash shook her head in wonderment.

For his part, Gabe elected to simply lay about the enemy troops with arms that had become massive broadswords. Then, without warning, he charged straight at a tank, and the soldiers in his path scurried to get out of his way.

Leaping high into the air—Ash took the opportunity to pelt Roach with her autocannons, but to little effect—Roach descended to pierce the tank with both blades.

He must have done something else to the tank, then, because it exploded beneath him. Moments later, Roach emerged from the conflagration to continue his rampage.

"What do we do now?" Beth said, her voice small.

"I don't know," Marco answered. "But I suspect it'll probably have something to do with dealing with *that.*"

Ash glanced toward Marco to see him pointing at the sky. She followed the gesture with her eyes.

Far above Eresos, hundreds of streaks of fire were hurtling toward the planet's surface. They were visible even in broad daylight.

"What is *that?*" Henrietta said.

"It's something entering the atmosphere," Ash said, remembering the way the Quatro mechs had first arrived on Eresos. "Many somethings, from the looks of it. And I doubt we're going to welcome our new visitors."

CHAPTER 44

Engage Together

"Captain," Ash said as Bronson answered her call, appearing on the ground before him. "Do you know anything about those meteorites that look like they're hurtling straight for us?"

Bronson rubbed his palms against both stubbled cheeks. "Ah. They showed up, then, did they?"

"Huh? What do you mean, 'they?' What are they?"

The captain sniffed. "I've been keeping the *Javelin* near the space elevator, hoping to intercept them there. I figured the elevator would be their first target...I knew they couldn't possibly move fast enough to race a destroyer accelerating at full power, but I never expected them to strike Vanguard..." The man cleared his throat.

"Would you mind telling me what the hell you're talking about, sir?"

Well, they're these little robots that nearly tore my hull clean off out in the Belt. Price had his hands full shooting them off the *Javelin* while battling the alien mech—"

"Wait, Jake fought one of those things?"

Shaking his head as though to clear it, Bronson said, "Look, Sweeney, all you need to know is that those things are small but vicious. They did a number on my ship's armor, and they'll do one on your MIMAS if you let them. So don't let them, all right?"

The dream-sky had turned blood-red to reflect Ash's anger. "Sir, if you knew about these things..."

"You have two entire battalions with you, Sweeney! Figure it out!"

With that, Bronson disappeared.

Unbelievable.

"Steam?" Henrietta said. "Are we just going to let this happen?" She was pointing at the alien mechs, whose killing sprees were still well underway.

"No," Ash said. "Actually, it looks like we're going to have to stop that, somehow, before those things in the sky arrive down here."

"What are those things, exactly?" Marco asked. They'd known Ash was contacting Bronson.

"Robots capable of ripping apart our mechs, apparently. From the sounds of it, facing them and the alien mechs at the same time is the last thing we want to do."

"So, we neutralize the three alien mechs first," Marco said. "How hard can that be?"

Ash glanced askance at him. She was used to sarcasm from Henrietta. If *Marco* had started being sarcastic, it was probably a good sign they were in trouble.

"We stick together," Ash said. "Remember how we took out the quad outside Ingress—by pinning it down and melting its armor with our lasers. All we have to do is take out the Quatro inside. So we focus on one of those first."

Since Roach no longer had a body they could kill, she had no idea how they'd put him down. She'd decided to concentrate on the enemy whose death she knew was at least possible.

Ash led the way across the battlefield, charging at the quad who'd strayed the farthest from the other two enemy mechs.

By now, the Darkstream formation *wasn't* one—instead, it was just a writhing mass that half-fled and half-fought, depending on a given unit's proximity to the hostiles.

Neither effort was going very well.

Hoping for the element of surprise, Ash charged at her target's backside, bayonets extended.

She should have known better. If the Quatro mech was anything like hers, its HUD would warn it of significant threats approaching from any angle.

Indeed, seconds before she drove her right bayonet into its metal hide, the quad turned, rearing up to crush her beneath metal paws.

Ash pivoted out of the way, retracting her segmented hands to fire up at the enemy mech as she sidestepped.

The moment the Quatro crashed back to the ground, Ash noticed Marco had leapt into the air, slowly flipping so that his mech's whole weight would be behind his blades when he fell.

The Quatro didn't seem to register the attack from above, and yet when Marco's bayonets drove home, they glanced off harmlessly, and he tumbled off the alien's hide to land in a heap.

The quad began to turn, but Henrietta was already there with her heavy machine gun, pelting the Quatro's head and lending a stutter to its movements.

Ash was still hung up on the ineffectiveness of Marco's attack. *Do the quads have a hardening mechanism of some sort?*

Maybe, if they had advance warning of a significant threat, they were capable of hardening their armor in that spot by compressing the metal scales there; trading versatility for impenetrability, for as long as they needed to.

It was the only way Ash could explain Marco failing to penetrate the quad with that much momentum behind his bayonets.

"We need to engage all at once, from four separate angles," Ash shouted over the team-wide. "I think it's able to turn away our bayonets if it knows they're coming, but if we can keep it guessing, surprise it..."

It was a long shot, but it was the best thing any of them had suggested yet.

Then again, it's also the only thing anyone's suggested.

Nevertheless, Oneiri moved to circle the quad, which in turn tried to isolate them and take them out one by one.

It charged Beth, and in the dream, Ash's distress took the form of the taste of cigarette ashes. She charged forward at the Quatro, bayonets extended before her.

The quad turned around, batting at Ash with a massive paw and sending her hurtling backward.

"What happened to engaging it together?" Henrietta said.

"Uh...right. Sorry."

They continued to circle the Quatro, trying out their entire arsenal on it.

At this range, their heavy machine guns seemed to have a good effect, opening gaping craters in the Quatro's metal hide that took a while to close.

Oneiri's assault on the quad had given the soldiers around them an opening to catch their breath and increase pressure on the quad as well.

Ash could tell the soldiers were well-trained: they took care to avoid hitting the **MIMAS** mechs, and their shots were well-timed, forcing the Quatro into compromising its position several times.

But nothing seemed to work. Either Oneiri was failing to get the drop on the quad or it had learned to repel their blades with a one-hundred-percent success rate.

If that's the case, we're doomed.

But she had to assume they would get there eventually.

We have to keep trying.

"Uh...Ash?" Marco said, his gaze fixed on a point beyond her.

Ash didn't have to ask what he was looking at, and when she patched through a feed from one of the visual sensors on her back, it confirmed what she feared: the first robots were starting to crash to the earth, their landing zones scattered across the empty expanse between them and the town. Great plumes of dust sprouted into the air with each impact, and each robot sprinted toward the Darkstream forces the instant it gained its footing.

They looked like tiny mechs, with limbs that were shaped like elongated shields and heads that curved forward as well as back.

And they ran like demons chased them.

"Sweeney," Bronson said, his likeness appearing suddenly on the hard-packed ground before her. "I may have a solution to the robot problem you're experiencing."

"Oh? That's welcome news."

"Well, I wouldn't exactly call it..." Bronson cleared his throat. "I've parked the *Javelin* in low orbit, directly over the battle. I have orders to, uh, nuke the entire area if things go south."

Ash froze in place, stunned, while the others grappled with the quad. "But...that'll kill the Darkstream forces as well, not to mention the citizens of Vanguard."

"If you're defeated, everyone there will die anyway. So don't lose, and it won't be an issue. Bronson out."

The captain disappeared from the battlefield outside Vanguard once more.

CHAPTER 45

Champion

Gabe's feet, ever-shifting to grant him perfect balance, pounded across the hard-packed dirt as he laid open devil after devil with his blades.

How many must I kill?

He'd intended the question rhetorically, but as they often did, the whispers offered up an answer:

All of them. You must kill them all. Only then will the location of your beloved be revealed.

Gabe swept a man's head off his shoulders with a flick of one of his broadswords, and the puny ball of flesh and bone sailed through the air trailing droplets of blood before falling to the hard-packed ground. Less than a second later, its body followed.

Most of the figures he slew seemed minuscule to him, and they offered him no challenge whatsoever. The stinging of their weapons had the same effect that hail had on human skin—it hurt a little, sometimes, but hail rarely killed anyone.

The tanks held more interest for him, actually providing some satisfaction whenever he succeeded in taking one out. The armored personnel carriers caught his eye, too, and he thought it would be enjoyable to make those explode, though the feat would hold little tactical value.

Besides, they might be keeping Jess in one of them.

He'd been ecstatic when the whispers told him that she was still alive. Or at least, he'd felt that way once they'd convinced him of it.

At first, he was been skeptical. He'd seen Jess's corpse with his own eyes—the scarlet that stained her white summer dress.

That wasn't her, the whispers insisted. *It wasn't her at all. They fooled you, Roach.*

But if it hadn't been Jess, then who?

No one, the whispers answered. *That was no one. They've been keeping you in a waking dream, Roach, and it is only now that you have entered* my *dream that you are awake.*

The whispers had explained it all: how Darkstream had fabricated the Ambler attack on Allendale, sending him north to investigate the hoax.

On the way, they'd hijacked his implant, sending him into lucid without his knowledge.

There, they'd concocted this whole fantasy: of the Quatro attacking Northshire, of them killing Jess Sweeney as well as her father and the other villagers.

Not that the Quatro were blameless—oh, no. They had helped Darkstream fool him, and they'd betrayed their own kind on top of that.

That was why he and the two quads had slaughtered human and Quatro alike, back in River Rock. No one liked being betrayed by your own kind, no matter the species.

A woman in his path stood her ground, showing no fear as she fired round after round from her SL-17 up into his face. Gabe was about to cut her down when he stopped, frozen on the battlefield, his rampage far from complete.

He asked the whispers a question he hadn't asked them before.

Why...why would Darkstream trick me into thinking Jess was dead? What would they stand to gain from that?

A high-pitched cackle rose up inside him, then, and he had to suppress the urge to clutch his head with his metal hands.

Gabriel Roach, must you really ask? Do your enemies need a reason for the evil they do, other than their evil natures? The laugh came again. *They did this because they are war profiteers. The humans and the Quatro both—they conspire to make their species fight, and after each battle they count their credits.*

"I see," Gabe muttered, and of course it all made sense, now. He should have seen it before. It brought him shame that he'd been foolish enough to have to ask.

Continue your slaughter, Roach. It is the same mission you've been on almost all your life. Kill, kill, kill. It doesn't matter who directs you to do the killing. It never has. Has it? Has it?

The whispers had become a single, unified shriek. Gabe returned to fighting.

He commanded his arms to transform from broadswords into rotary autocannons, and he sent streams of hot lead into all who stood against him.

As meteorites crashed to the earth all around him, becoming metal bipeds who also engaged the Darkstream forces, Gabe focused on one of the **MIMAS** mechs—the one with yellow swirls covering its face and body.

There, the voice inside him said, having become a whisper once again. *Kill her, and you will have your answer.*

"But how—"

That is their champion! Kill her, and your enemies will surely crumple! What can they do, then, but yield to you your beloved?

Gabe knew exactly who the whispers had instructed him to kill.

"Jess won't be happy with me..." he mumbled.

But if this meant getting her back, it was worth it. Anything would have been.

He charged.

CHAPTER 46

Makeshift Gunships

In short order, the twenty or so Quatro who charged at the enemy holding the canyon were mowed down in a hail of gunfire.

They lack military training.

To Lisa, that was clear. If they'd possessed the discipline instilled by training, they would never have let their emotions lead them to their own deaths.

She'd hoped that the Quatro's sheer size and ferocity would compensate for their lack of training, but now she began to doubt that.

I need to get them under control.

Suddenly, she remembered that her jumpsuit's collar had an amplification function, in the event that coms went down and shouting became the only means of communicating in battle. She used her implant to activate it.

"All units fall back in an orderly fashion! You infantry in front—go to the right or left of the Quatro you're retreating past!"

She wasn't sure "infantry" was quite the right term for the Quatro—they were more like cavalry than anything else. Some of them had been outfitted with spare guns Lisa's militia had had on the shuttles, making them...a mix between cavalry and infantry?

Now was not the time to puzzle over their classification. Bullets rained down all around her, sinking into Quatro flesh.

Rug positioned herself between Lisa and the robot army, and she saw the Quatro twitch as ordnance found its way into her body, her facial features contorting.

"Move out of the way, Rug!"

"I will not. You move back, out of harm's way. Fall back, Lisa Sato."

She let out a frustrated sigh through gritted teeth as she began striding backward, ducking out from behind Rug whenever she could to provide covering fire for their retreat. Her shoulder was killing her.

"Militia members and Quatro with guns," she barked, "return fire against the enemy units that are pressuring us most!"

The swiftness with which her soldiers followed her command pleased Lisa—and also brought her a small measure of relief.

Maybe this isn't completely hopeless after all.

Rug also turned around to fire on the enemy with the energy weapons strapped to her back, though she continued to provide physical cover to Lisa as she stalked backward.

At last, the majority of Lisa's force made it to cover. The uneven terrain was good for that, at least—there were plenty of hollows, hills, and short cliffs to use.

Even those who could find no cover were protected by the distance they'd put between themselves and the canyon, which was where the robots seemed intent on remaining.

"Tessa," Lisa subvocalized over a two-way channel. "What's your location?"

"Taking cover to the south."

"Looks like I was right about the robots organizing and opposing us."

"It seems you were," Tessa said after a short pause. "But I stand by what I said. There's no point in obsessing over something until it becomes an actual problem."

"Right. Well, it's a problem now. There must be satellite photos of the terrain to the north and south—have you had a chance to look at them? Is there another route we can take?"

"Doesn't look like it. According to these elevation readings, the land to the north is too variable to allow passage for a force of any meaningful size. To the south, mountains, with no discernible pass through to the west that I can make out." Tessa sighed. "I'll admit, it looks like these machines are clear on their goal: prevent us from returning west."

Lisa racked her brain for an answer that didn't involve trying to advance through that meat grinder.

We could ferry our forces back and forth using the shuttles...

But no, that was stupid. It would take weeks to move everyone, and they'd make themselves vulnerable to attack during the operation. Besides, they'd run out of fuel long before they transported everyone.

Somehow, I doubt Darkstream will be willing to lend us more.

At last, she said, "Tessa, do you see an alternative to battling through that canyon?"

"Not unless we leave the Quatro we've recruited behind. I'm assuming we don't consider that an option."

"I don't. Do you?"

"No."

"All right, then." Lisa stared over the sunbaked land, at the canyon that would be her crucible. "There has to be a way to get to the top of one of those cliffs that form the canyon. What are you seeing on the photos?"

"Uh...I'd try for the southern cliff—try to find a path through the mountains that leads to it. The mountain slopes look treacherous, and I'm not sure humans could get up there, but maybe Quatro could. *Maybe.*"

"I say we send Rug and the Alex Quatro with their energy weapons, plus half the Quatro we've outfitted with guns and another fifty without. Their mission will be to take that cliff and fire down on the robots in the canyon as well as the ones stationed on the opposite cliff. They can time the attack with our own charge at the canyon. What do you think?"

"Well, it's your call. You're in command. But if you ask me, it still sounds risky as hell. I think we can expect our forces to get torn to shreds as we try to take that canyon."

"Maybe not, if we order our ten shuttles to fly forward to join the fight. They're combat shuttles, remember? If we use them as makeshift gunships, order them to hit the robots from the air, and Rug and the others hit them from that cliff, we might just be able to make a go of this."

"Huh." Judging by the silence that followed that syllable, Tessa was mulling the plan over. "I sure can't think of anything better."

"Then we'll run with what we have. I'll start handing out the orders."

"I'll sit on my ass, I guess."

"No you won't. You'll organize the armed Quatro we're keeping with us, along with the humans from our militia. I want them spread out from each other as much as possible, to reduce their vulnerability to enemy fire and to increase the firing solutions they have on those metal bastards."

"Hey, someone taught you well."

"That someone had better get moving. Sato out."

CHAPTER 47

Concentrated Fire

Ash soon discovered the most efficient way to fight the robots that continued to fall from the sky.

She kept her hands retracted and settled against her wrists but left her bayonets extended. That way, she could rip apart the robots with armor-piercing rounds when they were far, and slash them to pieces or impale them when they were near.

"Keep both your bayonets and your autocannons deployed at all times," she ordered the others once she figured that out. "We have to keep them off our armor."

Though the robots looked fragile, and they certainly disintegrated in short order under concentrated fire from the rotary autocannons, they could do a lot of damage if they made it through. There was power in those little limbs, and Ash had a wicked gash down her right thigh, where circuitry was now visible and coolant had begun to leak out.

I won't let that happen again.

She'd integrated the dream's unique way of interpreting stimulus with the visual sensors that covered her mech, and whenever one of the robots attacked her from any angle, she developed an itch on the spot where it would hit, and the world flashed red in that direction.

One of the robots tried to come at her from the air, having leapt far overhead. Ash's head itched, making her wince at the image of the metallic creature digging into her brain, even though her actual head didn't reside inside her mech's.

Either way, her bayonet sliced the robot clean in two before it came anywhere near her.

Four more robots charged, having woven between nearby Darkstream units to take her by surprise. Two of them came from more or less the same direction, but the other two were spread out.

She picked off the pair near each other, impaled one that was headed for her chest, but failed to deal with the fourth before it latched onto her bicep and began to savage it.

Seizing it by its arm, she whipped it into the air while maintaining her grip, so hard that part of its body snapped off, sailing away over the battling robots and soldiers. She threw what remained in her hand as hard as she could at another robot about to reach her, which drove it back, buying her time to make it explode with her right autocannon.

The tide of combat granted her a brief reprieve, then, which she used to check on her teammates. Nearby, three robots were descending through the air toward Beth.

Ash spun up her autocannons, aiming at two moving targets simultaneously and taking them both down. As for the third,

Beth caught it in two cupped hands, then crushed the thing between metal palms.

"Thanks!" Beth said, turning to nod at Ash.

"Anytime," said Ash as she picked off another enemy headed for Beth, and her teammate shook one off that had begun to tear at her ankle with tiny metal claws.

"How are you holding up?" Ash asked.

"I've been better...though I guess this is what I signed up for."

"Fighting Quatro is what you signed up for. I can't decide whether this is better or worse."

Beth turned toward her, and something about the way she froze told Ash everything she needed to know.

"Ash, behind you!"

She'd already begun to turn—far too late, however.

A serrated blade made of dark metal sprouted from her chest, right where her body was nestled inside the MIMAS.

The dream washed everything she could see in a deep scarlet, through which she could make out only dim outlines.

The blade retracted, and Ash slumped to her knees. She fell forward, her face connecting with the hard ground.

CHAPTER 48

Everything at her Disposal

The dream rendered Beth's anguish by sending cracks through the sky from which bled the darkness of space, staining the blue surrounding them.

She charged at Roach, and he withdrew his blade from Ash to face Beth, massive arms folding inward to become energy cannons, which immediately began to crackle with light.

Too late.

Beth engaged her rockets, blasting into Roach's midsection and carrying him backward several meters to crash into the side of a tank, which shifted sideways under their combined weight.

Pushing off him with her feet, she surged forward once more to land a right hook on his jaw, then drove her bayonet as hard as she could into his midsection. It plunged through, hitting the tank on the other side.

Roach tried to seize her, but she darted backward, reaching behind her to disconnect her heavy machine gun and swing it around, riddling his chest and face with bullets.

Still, Roach plowed forward against the barrage, and she hit him with a pair of rockets at point-blank range.

Praying it had bought her enough time, Beth ran back to the spot where Roach had impaled Ash.

The robots had left Ash alone during Beth's brief absence, probably assuming she was finished. At first, Beth feared that too, and the thought almost buckled her knees.

But when she checked, she saw that Ash was alive, even though her vitals were awash with red.

Knowing the **MIMAS** was designed to keep its pilot alive for as long as possible, Beth didn't dear remove Ash from it. Instead, she bent and picked her up, balancing her atop her right shoulder while holding her heavy machine gun in her left hand.

The little metallic devils ran at her once again, and Beth picked them off with her heavy gun, one by one, swinging it wildly from target to target while keeping a firm hold of the gun to prevent it from slipping from her grip.

When the robots began to swarm her, she simply ran, firing behind her without looking.

Her objective was a shallow rise beyond the fighting, and when she reached it, she gently laid Ash down on her back.

With that, she turned back to face the oncoming robots, immediately sweeping her heavy gun back and forth across their ranks.

Not fast enough. There were dozens of the robots approaching at a full run, unflinching in the face of Beth's defense. More were joining the chase from the periphery of the battle, probably smelling easy meat. *Two for the price of one.*

Worse: the meteorites that contained the robots were still falling from the sky at regular intervals.

Beth tossed her heavy gun aside, since it would have taken too long to replace it on her back. Then she retracted both her hands to reveal her rotary autocannons. She opened fire.

The vibrations that the autocannons sent through her arms was a pleasant sensation for Beth, and she also liked the way they made her forearms spin around and around in tight circles.

It was even more satisfying when the sensation was paired with robot after robot disintegrating before her eyes.

But it still wasn't enough. Beth judged that the robots would reach the hill soon no matter how well she targeted them, and so she did the last thing she could think of that might prevent them from reaching Ash.

She offered herself to them as *their* target.

When she charged to meet them, the robots almost seemed to gain in speed, as though her approach had infused them with eagerness.

They threw themselves upon her as she ran among them—but she increased her speed, causing most of them to miss.

Two did manage to latch on to her; one on her calf, and one on the small of her back.

She kicked off the first, sending it careening into another robot as Beth's foot knocked a third flat on its back. But the remaining robot immediately set about burrowing into her mech, and Beth was forced to fall backward onto the ground, crushing it.

The others pounced on the opportunity, rushing toward her while she was down, but Beth was in the finest form of her life, driven by the intense fury that had risen within her after what Roach had done to Ash.

She snapped both her arms backward, just as she'd seen some of the robots do in order to launch themselves up at the mechs.

It worked—the maneuver sent her hurtling back to her feet, and she sliced through two more airborne enemies as she did, generating a storm of metal parts that rained down onto the dusty ground.

Whipping around, she punched another robot in midair before jogging backward toward the hill where Ash lay, opening fire on the remaining hostiles.

Yet more enemies emerged from the battle and fell from the sky, intent on destroying the two MIMAS mechs.

Beth refused to allow it. To protect Ash, she would use everything at her disposal—her wits, her training, her skill, and even her life, if it came to that.

CHAPTER 49

Instant Headache

"How close are you, Rug?" Lisa Sato asked.

"It is difficult to tell," Rug answered. "I have not laid eyes on my destination for some time."

"All right. Keep me posted. Sato out."

Rug was trying her best. As she led her force through the mountains, she kept in close touch with Lisa Sato using subvocalization, a function her translator enabled. To speak out loud would have risked warning the machines on the cliff of her approach.

Of course, that was provided she made it to the top of the cliff at all. Together, she and the twelve Quatro with her from Alex, as well as the sixty-five from the eastern drifts, had taken more than an hour to get even this far.

All the while, the Meddlers' machines bombarded Lisa Sato's position.

Rug knew that her human friend didn't think of the machines as such—as belonging to the Meddlers. She preferred to put their very existence out of her mind, as a distant, undefined possibility that she didn't have to deal with right now.

That was not an uncommon tendency, among both humans and Quatro. But it never failed to aggravate Rug immensely.

Lisa Sato did not endure the Meddlers' onslaught. She did not lose everything to them.

Still, Rug's friend was not stupid, and she had ordered her force back as soon as the machines had struck, saving most of her soldiers. Rug herself had taken two bullets, one in her shoulder and one in her right flank, which had entered at oblique angles and hadn't seemed to hit anything vital. She was able to navigate the treacherous mountain ways despite the pain caused by the bullets inside her.

Before turning the next corner, she checked around it, as she had with every turn so far. At last, she beheld the cliff.

Only one machine was there, but it was also one of the most fearsome machines Rug had ever encountered.

It was an Ambler.

Other than the fifty unarmed Quatro, she also had sixteen with energy weapons and fifteen with human guns. Rug felt reasonably confident she could take the cliff from the colossus. It would entail significant loss of life—possibly half her force or more.

But there was no other choice.

She sent the message of what she had seen back to the Alex Quatro, who were evenly dispersed throughout the force behind her, so that they could quickly disseminate to the others whatever news she gave them over their communicators.

Once her companions had been given time to steel themselves, there was nothing for it but to emerge.

Beyond the path she now exited, there was an expanse of perhaps one hundred and fifty meters until the plateau terminated at the cliff. That would afford their force space to arrange itself into some sort of attack formation, but Rug doubted they would have much time to do so. The Ambler would likely notice them forming up in short order.

Nevertheless, she crept from the path as quietly as she could, taking care to disturb no loose rocks as she padded across the ground, keeping as far from the Ambler as possible while giving those behind her room to emerge and begin arranging themselves.

Twenty Quatro—only three of them bearing energy weapons—had emerged when the Ambler finally turned, instantly opening fire with the heavy guns mounted on both its sides.

Though Amblers possessed the same ability to morph that the Gatherers did, they used it less, and certain components seemed essentially permanent, such as the long, heavy guns it now used to send streams of lead into Quatro flesh.

The seventeen unarmed Quatro who'd made it onto the plateau charged, with the four in front quickly falling to the Ambler's fire.

The felled Quatro crashed to their bellies, and Rug saw one Quatro's head glance off a sharp-looking rock. It pained her to see a mighty warrior lose his dignity in this way.

Rug opened fire herself, sending bolts of white light toward the Ambler's dome, where she assumed its "mind" resided—if indeed it had one. Either way, the dome offered the biggest target, and her efforts didn't take long to earn her the attention of the machine.

The Ambler turned lasers on her, and Rug immediately fled the spot she'd been standing, though heat had already begun to build up on top of her head, imparting an instant headache. A moment longer, and the temperature would have likely caused her skull to rupture.

The other two Alex Quatro opened fire on the enemy, granting Rug covering fire, and more armed Quatro now emerged onto the plateau to join in.

Perhaps this will go better than I'd assumed.

The mech seemed unable to focus on any one target long enough to neutralize it—the Quatro were succeeding in fragmenting its attention and preventing it from doing significant damage.

Then, one of her companions called out, and Rug recognized his voice as the one who'd imprisoned Lisa Sato and Tessa Notaras: "Look beyond, at the opposite cliff!"

Rug looked from Salve—which was the name the drift leader had chosen for himself—to the far cliff.

On it, two more Amblers pounded toward the edge.

Then, incredibly, they leapt into empty air.

Rug thought they must surely plummet to their doom—until rockets sprouted from their undersides, carrying them to the cliff where the Quatro fought. Both mechs crashed to their feet, flanking the Ambler already there and causing the ground to tremble.

Rug had never before heard of Amblers having that capability.

"Rug?" Lisa Sato's voice said, sounding alarmed. "Did I just see what I thought I saw?"

But there was no time for a response. A promising engagement had just become a losing one.

Rug surged forward to do what she could to help her fellow Quatro.

CHAPTER 50

Locked in Combat

Marco had seen Roach impale Ash, and he'd caught glimpses of Beth's attempts to protect her from the swarming robots.

But there'd been nothing he could do to help. He and Henrietta had been working together to engage one of the quads, to prevent it from killing more Darkstream soldiers.

Even that was getting a lot less of his attention than it deserved, since it took almost everything he had to keep the smaller robots from shredding his mech.

But when Marco saw Roach advancing on the hill where Beth carried on her desperate struggle to keep the robots from ravaging Ash's mech, he knew he *had* to do something.

So he charged, through the battling soldiers and robots, battering aside any enemy that got in his way while weaving around or leaping over friendlies.

"Spirit, where are you going?" Henrietta said, frustration giving her voice an edge. "We're making progress against this thing!"

They hadn't been, but Marco wasn't about to contradict her right now. "If Roach reaches that hill, both Steam and Paste are done. Paste already has her hands full with the robots."

When he saw that Roach was going to reach his target no matter how fast Marco ran, he sent two rockets streaming across the battlefield at the alien mech.

One missed, though it chanced to take out one of the smaller robots—and the other hit. It caused Roach to stagger a step, and then he whipped around to see who'd attacked him.

It worked...I got his attention!

But soon, Marco began to feel his gambit had worked a little *too* well. Roach dashed toward him, arms taking the form of broadswords, just as they had at the beginning of the battle.

Aware that if he hesitated at all, he was lost, Marco extended both his bayonets and charged as well.

As they neared each other, Roach positioned himself for an obvious thrust. So obvious, in fact, that Marco expected a feint, but he readied himself to parry it just in case Roach followed through.

Roach *did* follow through, and Marco raised his blade to intercept. It didn't go as planned. At the last second, Roach's broadsword had become a massive, metal fist, which shattered Marco's bayonet and connected with his chest, knocking him to the ground with shocking force.

Staring up at the sky, mentally shaking himself, he tried to get up.

That didn't work, either. Roach stepped forward, planting a heavy foot on Marco's chest while bringing his arms together.

Those arms melded, sending tendrils into each other to intertwine and twist around to become a single, gigantic energy cannon angled at Marco's head.

Lightning crackled inside that cannon.

"Say goodnight, Gonzalez," Roach said, and his voice sounded like that of the damned.

Something streaked out of the sky, the angle of its approach vector changing rapidly until it was almost parallel with the ground.

Just before it would have collided with the ground, it collided with Roach instead, knocking the alien mech off of Marco and sending it skidding, leaving deep furrows in the hard-packed earth to mark its passage.

Marco managed to regain his feet, and when he looked in the direction Roach had been carried, he saw that Roach's mech was locked in combat with its identical twin.

CHAPTER 51

Balance of Power

Jake slammed into Roach, driving him off of Marco—just in the nick of time, from the looks of it.

To avoid killing everyone on the battlefield, with the possible exception of the mechs, he'd devoted some effort to arresting the momentum he'd gathered from his atmospheric reentry.

Even so, he'd hit Roach with a lot of force, which carried them both several dozen meters across the ground.

Roach was beneath him, luckily, and it was his mech that took the brunt of the damage.

Part of Roach's mech slapped the ground, presumably in an attempt to slow their momentum, though the effect was that Jake tumbled forward instead, with Roach flipping around behind him and both of them rolling end over end, still locked together.

Finally, Roach managed to regain his feet, separating himself from Jake, though their forward motion caused them to skid several more meters. For a few seconds, they "surfed" over the hard-packed dirt.

As they slowed, Jake stepped forward and delivered a hay-maker to the base of Roach's throat, causing him to stagger backward, clutching at it with his right hand.

He seemed surprised by the force Jake was capable of bring-ing to bear—equivalent to the power Roach himself wielded.

"Not used to that, are you?" Jake asked.

"Who...who *are* you?"

"I'm the one who gave you that mech, you asshole."

Jake strode forward, converting his left hand into a heavy machine gun and firing at Roach's head over and over at point-blank range.

His former chief's response was to sidestep rapidly, clearly angling himself to strike Jake's back.

Jake let him complete the maneuver—and the moment Roach was in position, he repeated the trick he'd discovered in the Belt, inverting so that he faced backward without having to turn around.

The maneuver appeared to shock Roach, and the instant of hesitation made the hook Jake landed on his jaw all the more effective.

Roach stumbled backward once again. "Price," he spat, as though the name was a flea that had flown into his mouth.

"Good guess. You know, when I picked you up from your sickbed and carried you across Valhalla like a baby, to be born again inside that mech, I didn't expect *this.*"

The other mech shook its head slowly. "You..." Roach said, trailing off for a moment. "You truly don't understand what's happening here?"

Ignoring the question, Jake took the fact that they'd stopped to chat as an opportunity to turn his left arm into an energy cannon and blast Roach's head off.

At least, he tried. Roach sidestepped once again, and the energy glanced off his head, causing it to jerk violently but doing no significant damage.

Either way, it seemed to piss him off, since next, Roach tried to tackle him. Jake met the charge head-on, and they grappled for several moments without either one of them making any headway. They were virtually matched in strength.

But perhaps not in skill.

"The whispers...don't they call to you?" Roach asked.

That took Jake aback, and his shock was the window Roach needed to alter their engagement. He twisted forward, breaking Jake's grasp in order to deliver a savage headbutt.

This time, it was Jake's turn to stagger backward as he struggled to keep his feet under him. Roach ran forward to try to capitalize on the loss of balance, but Jake's arms became twin autocannons to send fragments of himself screaming toward Roach.

That, it seemed, was a mistake, as Roach merely absorbed the fragments, adding their mass to his own. Jake quickly stopped firing.

"The whispers should have explained to you the truth," Roach said as he took one inexorable step after another, his fists clenched, fingers writhing against each other. "They must call to you. The suit *must* whisper to you."

"It does," Jake said. "I'm just not stupid enough to actually listen."

It wasn't nearly that simple, of course, but the taunt had the desired effect of enraging Roach further, causing him to lose all restraint and charge at Jake with abandon.

Jake ran to meet him, but he dropped to the ground at the last second, sliding feet-first in an attempt to trip his enemy. To supplement the effort, he shifted his mass to make the alien mech more wedge-shaped, hoping to send Roach flying through the air so he could shoot him on the way down.

But Roach was transforming too—into a wheel with serrated edges, which ran over Jake, severing his right arm from his torso.

Flipping onto his stomach, Jake scrambled toward the limb, desperate to rejoin it with the rest of his body.

But Roach had assumed a humanoid form once more, and his foot connected with Jake's chin, sending him flipping backward, recoiling in pain.

He recovered just in time to watch Roach pick up the arm and hold it against his chest, where tendrils snaked out to embrace it. Within seconds, it had been absorbed into the alien mech.

CHAPTER 52

Full Potential

After Roach absorbed Jake's right arm into his chest, the battle became more challenging for him.

His actual arm was fine, of course—it was still attached to his body, anyway, inside the torso of his massive mech. But that wouldn't mean much if Roach killed him.

I don't see why I can't simply regrow the arm.

Indeed, as he focused on the jagged stump where his mech's arm had been, he felt an itching sensation within the mech dream.

But Roach wasn't about to wait around while Jake regenerated a limb. He was that much larger, now, and he swung a fist at Jake that was shaped like a hammer.

Dancing backward neutered the attack somewhat, but Roach still struck a glancing blow on Jake's chest.

His arm continued to sprout from his shoulder, though it was a thin, weak-looking thing, and it seemed it would take forever for it to regain its musculature.

How was Roach able to incorporate my arm so quickly? Jake commanded his left arm to become an autocannon, afraid that an energy gun would detract too much from the regeneration process. *The autocannon should hold him off for a bit...*

The dream flashed scarlet—just before one of the quads tackled him from behind, knocking him onto the ground and pinning him there.

The insects that had haunted Jake back in Hub returned, then, digging into his flesh with more vigor than ever before. The single, grating violin note returned as well.

Let us join as one, the alien mech whispered to him. *Only then will you be granted full command of your abilities.*

"No," Jake grunted, and four pillars shot out of his body and into the ground, jostling the Quatro mech enough to allow him to roll onto his back and place his autocannon against its underside.

He fired, and the rounds sank into the quad's belly.

The Quatro spun away, emitting a strangled roar. It seemed Jake might have actually gotten a shot through to the beast inside. He didn't know how he'd managed it, but the thing certainly seemed rattled.

His arm had continued to grow, and now he told his other arm to become a long, thin blade, with which he was determined to lay open the quad who'd attacked him.

The other quad charged, then—but this time, Jake was ready. He sidestepped the alien, jamming his left arm backward as he went so that it tore through the thing's armor.

Rapidly, he reformed the autocannon, intent on sending high-velocity rounds into the rift he'd made—

Roach tackled him, then, and they flew through the air to land on the ground. Straddling Jake, Roach gripped him by the neck, pulled him upward, then punched him so that his head slammed back into the hard-packed dirt. Roach repeated the act once. Twice.

I can't take on all three of them at once.

The whispers answered immediately, this time: *You can. You are better than them, and once you are on equal footing, you will tear them apart. Let us join as one.*

This time, Roach's fist sprouted spikes before crashing into Jake's face. Metal fragments flew, reminding him of the Ravagers who'd torn apart his face back in the Belt.

He couldn't find the purchase to throw Roach off, or to wriggle out from underneath him. His adversary was larger than him, now, and it seemed absorbing the arm had lent him more power, too.

Let us join as one, the alien mech whispered.

Almost, Jake did it. The only alternative seemed to be death, for him and his friends.

Okay. I'll...

The dream seemed to sing in anticipation, and a second note joined the lone violin note, to create a hauntingly beautiful harmony. Roach's fist slammed into Jake's head again.

But then he remembered Sue Anne's gaunt face, staring up at him from her deathbed, holding his gaze riveted.

Remember me, Jake. Remember me, fighting to live despite how badly I wanted to die. I want you to remember how much you owe me. How deeply in debt you are to me—a debt you can never, ever repay, except by continuing to resist that voice, forever.

"I deny you!" Jake yelled, and his voice boomed over the battlefield. "*I deny you!*"

With that, his right arm surged from his shoulder, metal sinews and tendons wrapping around it to lend it the mass it once had.

Jake used the regrown arm to grip Roach by the neck, and with a titanic effort, he slammed his adversary to the ground beside him, flipping over to become the one straddling Roach.

His left hand morphed, becoming an energy cannon, and he allowed the energy to build up for several seconds while Roach attempted to buck him off. Almost, the former chief succeeded.

Too late.

The cannon unleashed a broad, white-hot bar at point-blank range, taking Roach's head clean off. Where it had been remained only a melted stump.

One of the Quatro charged Jake, then, trying to take advantage of his diverted attention, but his newly formed right arm became a lance, which flickered like lightning toward the quad's chest, biting through the metal.

Judging from the way the enemy mech slumped to the ground, the lance had found the Quatro inside. Jake rose to his full height to face the remaining quad, but it turned to sprint toward the horizon as fast as it could.

A ragged cheer rose up from what beleaguered Darkstream soldiers were left over from the battle.

The cheer abruptly fell off into shocked silence, and Jake turned to find Roach's headless mech rising to its feet, both arms rapidly becoming energy cannons.

Incredible.

Jake turned his own energy gun into an autocannon, which took less time than forming weapons from scratch, as Roach was doing.

That done, he fired into Roach's right cannon, generating an explosion that took out the weapon.

As Roach staggered back from that attack, Jake surged forward to drive his lance into his enemy's remaining energy cannon.

There was a colossal detonation of heat and light that threw Jake back several meters to crash to the earth, his ears ringing, the violin note reaching a crescendo.

Blindly, he staggered to his feet, stumbling toward where he thought he would find Roach, though he couldn't see a thing.

He located Roach's mech by feel, and he realized through touch alone that both his adversary's arms now ended at the elbows.

He seized Roach's neck once more with his left hand and turned his right into a short sword, which he used to stab Roach over and over until the man's mech was a perforated wreck and he'd stopped moving altogether.

Only then did Jake allow his vanquished enemy to fall to the ground.

CHAPTER 53

Surge Forward

Lisa ran from shallow cliff to hollow to boulder, taking as little time as she could behind each hide before checking to ensure the way forward was clear and darting out again.

There's no way Rug and the others can hold out against three Amblers for long.

She knew that, and her friend would know it, too. But Rug and the others with her fought on, with ferocity and bravery. It would amount to a terrible betrayal for Lisa to squander the short window they'd granted her.

"How long till you engage?" she subvocalized to Planter, the Quatro she'd put in charge of the combat shuttles.

"Minutes, Lisa Sato. We will arrive in time to strike together."

That was the best she could have hoped for. With Rug engaging the Amblers who'd been firing on her force from the cliffs, Lisa would get a tiny window to strike the robot army within the canyon, and during that time they would be on more or less equal footing.

Other than the machines they have positioned partway up the cliffs, of course.

Those would likely pose a problem, but hopefully the combat shuttles could manage to pick most of them off.

Once the Amblers finish off Rug's force, though...

It tore her apart to consider the fact of Rug's impending death, but she *had* to consider it, because it would leave the Amblers free once again to fire down from the cliffs with their vast arsenals. Quite likely, they'd be able to take down the shuttles as well.

Lisa and her Quatro force, along with the four surviving humans under her command...together, they advanced forward under cover for as long as they could. Without the Amblers firing down on them, that ended up being a fair distance, since the Gatherers in the canyon didn't have long-range weapons.

Lisa had also spotted humanoid robots, a little shorter than an average person, though those didn't seem to have long-range weapons either.

There were two more Amblers inside the canyon, however, and they were picking off Quatro careless enough to expose themselves at an alarming rate.

At last, Lisa's force reached the canyon, and the swarm of Gatherers and bipedal robots chose that moment to surge forward as one, rapidly closing the distance.

The unarmed Quatro surged forward to meet them, and from behind, the armed soldiers fired on the robot host.

There are too many of them.

Even with the combat shuttles about to arrive, Lisa simply couldn't see how they'd pull a victory out of this situation.

But that didn't mean she didn't intend to try.

From atop a shallow rise, she took aim at one of the Gatherers about to close with a Quatro, then fired.

An Ambler spotted her, sending a rocket her way, and she dove off the hill, sprinting toward a nearby hollow for cover.

CHAPTER 54

Torn Asunder

A line of armor-piercing rounds hit Rug's rear-right leg, shearing through flesh and bone.

The pain made her roar in agony, but she continued moving toward the boulder she'd chosen for cover, the leg dragging uselessly across the ground.

More bullets tore up the boulder as she dove behind it. But she couldn't let herself rest.

Instead, she wended around the massive rock to fire at her attacker from the other side, blasts of energy forcing the Ambler back momentarily.

It recovered, answering Rug's efforts with a rocket. That forced her to scamper back, abandoning the rock but keeping it between her and the Ambler, her leg sending shockwaves of pain through her all the while.

The other Quatro on the cliff were in states similar to hers—the ones that survived, anyway. Most of the unarmed Quatro had been killed during the first minutes of battle, and now it was everything the armed Quatro could do to keep the three giant mechs occupied while remaining alive themselves.

"Rug, how's it going up there?"

"Not very well, Lisa Sato," she answered, glad that subvocalization allowed her to keep the agony out of her voice.

"Actually, you're doing amazingly, Rug. I never expected to have this much time to fight the battle on the lower ground."

"Thank you...but I do not think you will have much longer. I apologize. It has...been good to be your friend."

Part of her expected Lisa to tell her not to talk like that, but she only said, "I've cherished our time together too, Rug."

She also expects me to die this day.

Rug decided that if she was going to die, then it would be a good death.

She limped from the boulder she'd taken cover behind, pelting the nearest Ambler with bolt after bolt of energy.

It turned toward her, taking its attention from the pair of Alex Quatro it had been pinning down.

Those Quatro now emerged from cover too, joining their fire with Rug's.

Perhaps if we can take down just one Ambler, it could make a difference...

But the Ambler who'd nearly shot off her leg turned its rockets on her once more, and Rug knew it was over.

Suddenly, a streak of dark metal charged past her from the direction of the mountain pass they'd taken to get here. It leapt into the air, connecting with the Ambler, and the enemy's rockets were diverted to the mountainside beyond Rug.

"My soul?" she said, disbelieving.

The Quatro mech pushed off the Ambler, sending it tottering toward the cliff, and her mate hammered it with high-velocity rounds until it toppled, careening over the side to crash down to the battle below.

He turned on the next Ambler, which was already peppering him with its heavy guns.

Rug rushed forward to join her mate, sending bolt after bolt to slam into the Ambler's dome.

Her mate turned, and her eyes locked onto his robotic, glowing ones.

"Goodbye, my love," he said.

"My soul—no!"

With that, her mate rocketed up into the Ambler, knocking it off the cliff and sending them both flying from it.

Her heart torn asunder, Rug nevertheless banded together with the Quatro that remained on the cliff, and together they managed to neutralize the third Ambler. Their concentrated energy fire sent it to its knees, and then to the ground, where it slumped sideways and did not rise.

She and the other Quatro sprinted to the cliff side, then, to pelt the enemy robots in the canyon below.

"Rug!" Lisa said, excitement filling her voice. "The battle's turning in our favor. How did you manage to take out those Amblers?"

"We received some unexpected assistance," Rug said, and Lisa did not request clarification.

Perhaps she had been engaged by an enemy robot.

Or, perhaps, she'd heard the unbearable sadness in Rug's voice, and knew it was best not to question further.

The Demands of War

"That's no dust storm," Billy Overton said, his thumbs tucked behind his belt.

Jake glanced over at the old man, who squinted out over the Barrens, studying the oncoming formation. "You don't think so?"

"Nah. Dust storms come in like giant, puffy clouds rising up from the ground. This dust-up's narrower—high, and sharp. Reminds me of the day those Quatro mechs came, and another mech like the one you drive fought them. You might want to get in yours, boy."

Jake nodded. "I have time."

"S'pose you do, at that." Overton wrinkled his nose as he peered out over the land. "They're not coming as fast as they did on the day Sable Hawthorne died. I tried to warn the others that day, but you think they'd listen to me? Then, later on, those mechs all came back, the four-legged ones and the two-legged one, but this time they were working together to kill everyone. Billy had his shelter, though. Billy had his shelter." The last words came out as a mutter.

"Do you miss your neighbors, Billy?"

Abruptly, Overton's head sank, his chin settling against his chest. "Yeah," he said, and his voice hitched.

Something about the endearing gesture got to Jake—resonated with him. He laid a hand on Overton's shoulder. "I'll go get my mech."

"All right, then."

According to Beth, Oneiri had found Overton in River Rock soon after the second attack on it. They'd tried to persuade him to accept an evac out of the town, but he'd kicked up such a massive stink that the soldier dealing with him simply gave up and told Overton he could do whatever he wanted.

Darkstream had taken Ash to Valhalla Station to recover after the battle at Vanguard, along with Roach's remains, and the quad's.

Jake didn't think that seemed like a good idea—to hold on to what was left of the alien mechs for study. But it hadn't been his call to make.

Ignoring Bronson's order for Oneiri to return to Valhalla for a debriefing, though—that *had* been Jake's call.

It was all of our call.

They'd come here instead, to River Rock, to talk about the data dump Beth had given him, which Ash had received from the leader of Red Company. And also to discuss whether they wanted to work for Darkstream at all anymore.

The alien mech sat outside Overton's shelter, slightly slumped, as though lacking the life force that animated it when Jake was inside it.

That thing's like a sword with no hilt. It was a sharp sword, though, and it got the job done if you could resist its siren call.

Which he was determined to continue doing. Sue Anne's voice was too loud in his ears to do otherwise.

When Jake returned to Overton's side, there was a new gleam in the old man's eyes as he beheld the mech.

He likes tech—there's no denying that. Jake couldn't blame him. He did, too. Always had.

Soon, what Overton had called a dust-up resolved into a force of hundreds of Quatro.

As soon as it did, Jake opened a team-wide channel. "Inside your mechs, everyone. We've got company. Lots of it."

The three MIMAS mechs currently in operation joined him on the border of the Barrens minutes later. They managed to persuade Billy Overton to watch whatever happened from his shelter, though he wanted badly to stay and see it with his own eyes.

At last, the Quatro force neared, and two humans walked at their fore—a young Korean woman as well as a woman of Western descent, who looked like she must have been in her sixties at least, though she clearly didn't let her age slow her down very much.

"That's Lisa Sato and Tessa Notaras," Henrietta said. "Traitors. They killed Darkstream soldiers on Alex."

Henrietta was the least convinced about quitting Darkstream, and she'd taken a lot of persuading to come here at all—only her loyalty to Oneiri Team had swayed her to ignore Bronson's order long enough to join the discussions.

At hearing the names Henrietta had spoken, Jake breathed a sigh of relief. "There doesn't need to be any fighting."

Henrietta shot him a look. "Huh?"

"You three wait here." Jake strode out over the Barrens to meet the oncoming force.

"Whoa, there, big boy," Tessa Notaras said, leveling an assault rifle at him.

Cute. Jake held up his hands. "I surrender."

When he spoke, Lisa Sato stared at him, hard. "I recognize that voice. Could it truly be...?"

Jake opened his mech, a panel in front stiffening then lowering to make a ramp for him to descend.

When he reached the bottom, he gave a little wave. "Hi, Lisa."

She ran to him, her boots stirring up little puffs of dust as she did.

When she collided with him, she nearly knocked him back onto the metal ramp, and her embrace tightened hard over his frame.

He hugged her back. "Whoa. You've gotten stronger since the last time we were caught wrestling in Percival Brown's corn field."

She drew back from him, still holding both his arms. "Hi, Stink."

Wincing, Jake said, "I was hoping you'd forgotten that nickname."

He got inside his mech to take it back to River Rock, and they walked side-by-side, instantly launching into a dozen different memories about growing up in the Belt.

"I can't believe you're here," Jake said, peering down at her. "Last I heard, you'd taken a job on Alex. I was so jealous when I learned about that."

That made Lisa's smile shrink and grow tight. "It didn't end well."

"I heard that, too. I'm sorry."

He happened to glance behind him, and then he stopped walking altogether. A quad had caught his eye, marching at the periphery of the host.

"That's Rug," Lisa said. "She's a friend."

"I see," Jake said slowly. "Sorry…I'm used to fighting those things."

Lisa nodded. "Her mate piloted that mech, just a few days ago. He died, but the mech repaired itself."

They reached River Rock, and the three remaining MIMAS pilots were waiting for them on the village green. None of them had gotten out of their mechs.

To show them everything was all right, Jake opened his own mech and got out.

"Hey, guys, it's okay," he said. "We're among friends."

"Sorry," Henrietta said, leveling a finger at the multitude of Quatro, most of which remained just outside the village for now. "I don't remember agreeing to include a bunch of Quatro in our talks."

"We haven't even settled on what we're doing yet, Razor. Depending on what we decide, these Quatro could prove to be valuable allies."

"I don't side with Quatro, *Jake*," she countered. "And the fact that you're considering it frankly disgusts me."

Jake sighed. "I'm inclined to believe Darkstream really did provoke them. Hell, Bronson ordered me to abandon my own family to their deaths. And they would have died, along with almost everyone I've ever known, if I hadn't disobeyed to return to Hub."

Lisa shot him a sharp glance at that, her eyes wide and full of questions.

"Sorry, Jake," Henrietta said. "This isn't what I signed up for. If we're welcoming these Quatro instead of fighting them, then I'm out for good."

"I am, too," Beth said.

Jake shook his head slowly. "For real, Paste? You too?"

"Yeah."

Both MIMAS mechs turned and walked out of River Rock. A weight settled over Jake's heart as he watched them go.

He turned toward Marco. "How about you, Spirit?"

Marco's mech shifted its weight. "I'm with you, Clutch. Always."

"Good. Thank you." And it *was* good, but it also seemed like Oneiri Team was no more. The team had been shattered, and now they would be nothing more than separate agents fighting on opposing sides.

"Are we just gonna let them walk away?" Tessa Notaras said, gesturing at the departing mechs. "If we don't neutralize them now, we'll only face them on the battlefield."

"Yes, we are, Ms. Notaras," Jake said. "And yes, we probably will face them. But they were my teammates, and I won't dishonor them by gunning them down from behind."

"Then you're no soldier," Notaras said. "You're a fool."

"Maybe I am," Jake said, nodding. "Maybe this will come back to haunt me. But the members of Oneiri Team...we risked our lives for each other, countless times over. There are some codes that not even the demands of war should be permitted to break."

Acknowledgments

Thank you to Rex Bain, Inga Bögershausen, and Jeff Rudolph for offering insightful editorial input and helping to make this book as strong as it could be.

Thank you to Tom Edwards for creating such stunning cover art.

Thank you to my family - your support means everything.

Thank you to Cecily, my heart.

Thank you to the people who read my stories, write reviews, and help spread the word. I couldn't do this without you.

About the Author

Scott Bartlett was born 1987 in St. John's, Newfoundland, and he has been writing since he was fifteen. He has received various awards for his fiction, including the H. R. (Bill) Percy Prize, the Lawrence Jackson Writers' Award, and the Percy Janes First Novel Award.

In 2013, Scott placed 2nd in Grain Magazine's Canada-wide short story competition and in 2015 he was shortlisted for the Cuffer Prize. His novel *Taking Stock* was also a semi-finalist in the 2014 Best Kindle Book Awards.

Scott mostly writes science fiction nowadays, though he's dabbled in other genres.

Visit scottplots.com to learn about Scott's other books.